OTHER PEOPLE MANAGE

OTHER PEOPLE MANAGE

Ellen Hawley

SWIFT PRESS

This paperback edition first published by Swift Press 2023
First published in Great Britain by Swift Press 2022

1 3 5 7 9 10 8 6 4 2

Text designed and set in Minion by Tetragon, London
Printed and bound in Great Britain by CPI Group (UK) Ltd, Croydon, CR0 4YY

A CIP catalogue record for this book is available from the British Library

ISBN: 978-1-80075-099-9
eISBN: 978-1-80075-098-2

For Ida

1

BACK when Peg was still alive, back when we were both so young that neither of us was going to die, she told me about the five stages of grief. We'd each lost a parent when we were young – her father when she was fourteen; my mother when I was twelve – but even so we talked as if grief was something neither of us knew personally. This was in the seventies. The five stages were exciting and new, and that was all we let them be in that moment: something she'd studied in one of her classes; something we could talk about. When I try to remember the stages now, I come up with denial, bargaining, something else, another something else and acceptance. No matter how often I come back to fill in the blanks, I can't name the missing stages, and that seems oddly right. I live in one of those empty stages. Denial didn't work, there's nothing left worth bargaining for, and

I'm damned if I'll accept it. If I did, would Peg come back and drink that last cup of coffee with me after supper? That gap, that missing step, suits me.

Maybe it's the don't-care stage. The federal building gets blown up in Oklahoma City and I should care but no part of me really believes it matters. O.J. Simpson goes on trial, but his wife's murder is nothing beside Peg's death. If half the country was sinking into the sea, I might care, but only enough to make sure I was on the part that sinks.

I haul myself up off the couch, feeling the force of gravity working very personally against me. It doesn't want me upright. It wants me slammed flat against the planet, and that doesn't look like a bad place to be, really – it's natural, it's nonpolluting, it's organic. But I promised myself I'd go through Peg's clothes today. That's what you do when you're flattened by gravity and by grief. You set yourself tasks. You set goals. Get out of bed. Go to work. Wash the dishes. Wash the car. Take the clothing that once belonged to the person you've loved best in your life and give it to people who never knew she lived and don't give a shit that she's dead. Reach your hand down your throat, tear your heart out, and throw it onto the fast lane of the I-94. The five stages of grief. One, two, five. Time's up. Move on.

I sigh, releasing air and some tiny fraction of the pressurized regret that lives inside me, and I start up the stairs, feeling the light stab of my left knee each time it lifts me from one step to the next. I've always been big – tall, wide, solid, easily the size of most men – and it took me a long time to come to terms with my size. Now that I have, finally, wouldn't you know my knees have developed opinions of their own.

Peg's clothes are in the spare room, opposite the bedroom we shared. The house was built when people owned less stuff, when one narrow closet to a bedroom was plenty, thanks, so Peg hung her clothes in the spare room, leaving me the more convenient closet, and it's only now that I notice this, and notice that I never thought to say thanks, just hung my clothes up like that was my right. I thought of myself as the person who took care of her, and didn't notice the things she did for me. I have an impulse now to move them all, Peg's clothes to my closet and mine to Peg's. For the sake of balance, maybe. Or penance. Or to improve my character now that there's no one left in the world worth improving it for.

I open the closet and stand with one hand on the frame and one on the door, and I can't think what to do next. Under my hands is the woodwork we stripped and stained when we first bought the house, scraping off layer after layer of paint, the chemical stripper eating through our rubber gloves until we stopped wearing them, and who can say it wasn't that decision, to unearth the original woodwork, that ended up killing Peg.

On the floor is a neat row of Peg's shoes, toes pointing past me into the center of the room, and hanging from the bar, all neat and ready to put on, are Peg's clothes – the blacks and olive-greens and wine-reds that Peg liked to say didn't show stains so she wouldn't have to admit that she looked good in them, and knew that she did. Things that seem so important when there's a person to walk around inside the clothes and that don't matter a damn when there isn't. How strange that Peg owned this stuff, cared about this stuff, and then left me stuck with it all when she died. The wire hangers poke stiff corners into the shoulders of her shirts, making them too thin and too lonely to touch, but I do manage to take a hand away from the woodwork and set it on Peg's jacket, which is on a hook inside the door instead of pretending to drape around a body. It's one of those fuzzy fall-weight things, thick under my fingers, and comforting. I gather it against my face, thinking first, *This is a very odd thing to do*, and then, half by way of agreement and half by way of disagreement, *This is grief.* I don't weep, but it does seem like I should at least want to. What I feel, though, is nothing – absence, blankness, emptiness. I half hope Peg left a whiff of herself behind, but after she stopped burning incense I never associated any particular smell with her. What I smell here is nothing more personal than cloth and staleness. The smell of Peg's absence. I let the jacket's weight fall back onto its hook, fish a wadded kleenex out of one of its pockets, and raise it first to one eye and then to the other, blotting them before they have time to leak. The texture is woody and stiff. I imagine the germs of some long-forgotten cold pulling themselves out of dormancy and swimming across the watery surface of my eyes, struggling upstream through the tear ducts to reproduce in perfect detail a set of symptoms I can't remember Peg suffering through. If cancer could be caught this way, I'd still hold the kleenex to my eyes and offer myself as a host. Not because I'm hungry for death but because I'm not attached to living anymore. And because this is the closest I've felt to Peg since she died.

When I first met Peg, she had an ex, a three-night stand who was still standing, that first night, at the edge of the Women's Coffeehouse dance floor. The Coffeehouse was less a place to drink coffee than one of the few places where two women could dance together, and the ex's eyes followed every move Peg and I made. She was a small woman, the ex was – short, slight, neatly put together. If looks are what decide these things, she could have found someone else, she didn't have to let her life freeze at the moment Peg left her. That was all I registered about her that first time: small, not bad-looking, no real threat.

"I know it sounds paranoid," Peg said during a slow number. "The thing is, she follows me. It makes me completely crazy."

She had her arms around my neck and we were swaying more or less in time with the music. Neither one of us danced well, but some signal had passed between us, something that neither of us had under control, and dancing was the way to keep the connection open. Who knows why these things happen. It was the right time. We were the right people. On my side, some switch had flipped not long before I met Peg, and at thirty it hit me that I wasn't going to be eighteen for the rest of my life, and it made me understand that I was lonely. Even this soon after I met her, I understood that she had something solid about her, something I could trust. And she had an energy, as if she could make anything she looked at matter. If dancing was the way to keep her looking at me, I was happy to dance. Her hands rested on my shoulders, we swayed back and forth, and I felt like I hadn't really been alive until that moment. I'd been whacked by the universe's magic hammer: Clonk, you are now fully conscious and streaming with joy, and so it will stay for ever and ever amen.

Beside us, a couple was doing spins and dips and actual dance steps while Peg and I swayed in place. The taller woman had a tight-cropped Afro and gorgeous cheekbones, and the shorter one had red hair that flowed past her waist. They were stunning, both together and separately, and they danced like they'd known it all their lives. They were Coffeehouse regulars, and anytime they weren't dancing they were leaning toward each other across one of the tiny tables that lined the walls, as if they could hardly stand to let a slab of wood separate them. Week after week I struggled not to stare at them, but they were so damn beautiful that I stared anyway.

"Ignore her," I said in the direction of Peg's ear, talking not about the couple but the ex. "Let her watch if she wants to." Because I thought I understood the situation. Because our purest ignorance comes to us in the form of answers and certainty. The dance floor was crowded and I slid us toward the center, away from the ex, away from the couple with the beautiful looks and the dramatic relationship and the fancy dance steps. I couldn't imagine anyone preferring to watch us when they were around. The solution was so simple.

Hey, bring your problems to Margie. She solves them all.

Peg came up to my shoulder and she was round and comfortable to hold. She also had a voice that had gotten caught behind her nose somehow, making it too small and too silly for the person she was, but when you're first in love it's all charming. Later, if you're still in love, you stop noticing. It was Peg's voice. It made me happy to hear it.

We didn't talk about the ex anymore that night, and we didn't talk about her later that week, when Peg invited me out for coffee. She told me about school instead – about the five stages of grief, in fact – over banana cream pie and coffee at the Lincoln Del. She was working on a master's degree in social work and already, as an intern, working as a therapist. Later, when we'd been together for a while and I could see her as human-sized, she told me social work was the budget option. If she'd gone into psychology, she'd have needed a PhD before she could do anything useful, but all I heard at the time was "therapist", and I must have let what I was thinking show on my face, because she laughed and said it was okay, she couldn't read minds. I believed her enough to lie and say I hadn't thought she could.

I caught a glimpse of her right then as if I'd been sitting across the room, admiring a stranger. She was happy, she was smart, she knew the secrets of the human soul. She lived a life that was larger, deeper and more intense than mine. Except for the voice, life had been kind to her. If I hadn't been sharing her table, tucked inside the glowing circle of her knowledge and her luck, I'd have envied her for all of it. I couldn't see why she'd chosen me but I wasn't going to argue.

I'd started driving bus just a few months before I met Peg, and since not many women drove buses then, I used that to show off to her. I told her that sitting behind the wheel made me feel as if I was strong enough to bench-press the bus itself, all thirty thousand pounds of it. And I did usually feel that way, but I couldn't help comparing what I did to a master's degree, to her work as a therapist, and everything I was saying flattened out even before I said it.

"I know it's not rocket science," I said.

"It beats hell out of working in an office. And I'm willing to bet it pays more."

"I never did office work."

That launched her into a story about having worked for an advertising agency that refused to fix a half-busted typewriter until she threw it off the desk and shattered the plastic housing.

"They replaced it," she said. "Right after they replaced me."

We laughed about that. You let enough time go by, you add some caffeine, some sugar, a new relationship, and the next thing you know losing a job is a riot. Outside the window the snow lay two, maybe two and a half feet deep, but we were caffeinated and sugared and warm. I was sitting with someone who'd tossed a typewriter off a desk on purpose.

The talk got softer from there. She talked about her father, I talked about my mother, and our losses formed a link: we had these holes in our lives. I don't know what she believed, but I was sure we could fill them for each other. I'd found love. History would stop now. There was nothing left to record. We would be happy forever after. So I told her about my father's dark, airless house, and about his silences. I didn't tell her that sometimes, more than ten years after I'd last set foot inside it, I still had moments when I felt like that house was going to drag me back, when I'd have to work sense by sense to convince myself that the world was richer than my father had ever let himself know. I'd taste, smell, touch, notice, stretch my hand out and move some small object from one place to another and tell myself, *See, I can always change something.* I wasn't exactly hiding those times from Peg. They fell away from me right then as if they'd never happened.

In exchange for my father's house, she told me about her own father, who spent fifteen years working at a job he hated, trapped there by bills, by kids, by an accumulation of seniority, by the conviction that nothing else would be any different. In the last week of his life, when he couldn't get out of bed without help and reality had gone halfway liquid on him, he was trying to punch the clock one last time, begging Peg to help him find his time card. She told me about the kids she'd grown up with, who were punching clocks themselves by now, and knee-deep in babies and bills of their own. She didn't say that was what she was running from, but

I understood it all the same. We were both in flight.

She leaned toward me across the table and her face went soft with some memory.

"My father—" she said.

She didn't go on right away, just let her eyes track off into the distance, and I understood that she'd loved her father, and that she missed him.

"He used to sing. Not like perform or anything. It was just something he did when his mind was someplace else, but he had this really lovely tenor."

We smiled at each other, holding one conversation about our parents and a separate, silent one about ourselves.

"He had this one song that I never heard anyplace else."

I nodded. In another moment I'd have said, *I wish I could have heard it.* The conversation was slow-moving, full of pauses and gaps where we could look at each other, or look away. It left me time to turn my words over in my head and learn their shapes before I said them. I wasn't in a rush to get them out.

Before I said those particular words, though, Peg pulled herself up a notch and started to sing. In the middle of the Lincoln Del, with people at the other tables clinking their forks against their plates and the waitresses ping-ponging back and forth with coffee and ketchup, with all that bare open space around us and the windows staring out onto a Minnesota winter, she held my eyes and fuckin' well sang to me, an old-fashioned, scrolling kind of song in her small, trapped voice, not whispering the words the way I would have but *singing* them, with as much assurance as if she'd had her father's pure tenor.

> Come, my beloved, haste away,
> Cut short the hours of thy delay;
> Fly like a youthful hart or roe
> Over the hills where spices grow.

The clinking of dishes and the conversations around us died down. A waitress stopped near the kitchen door and stared at us. Someone clapped a few times, then stopped when no one else joined in, and a man behind Peg said – louder, I think, than he meant to – "Sweetheart, don't give up the day job."

The woman he was sitting with made an angry, shushing sound at him but Peg laughed as if he'd given her a standing ovation. She turned in her seat to call "Don't worry" in his direction.

When she turned back to me, she was still grinning. "I didn't inherit his voice," she said. "As you might've noticed."

How could I not be in love?

"You know, what I wish I'd asked is where he learned that song, what the story behind it was, because he wasn't a come-my-beloved kind of guy. But you don't think of things like that. Not till it's too late. And I'd gotten to the age where it embarrassed me, his singing. Where anything my parents did embarrassed me. I wish I'd had the chance to let him know that – you know."

I nodded, not because I did know but because I wanted to, and because that seemed like enough.

"That I'd remember it," she said. "That I'd carry it with me."

That weekend we went to a movie and then to Peg's place for coffee. She lived in one of those big Victorian houses that had been chopped into cheap, odd-shaped apartments, and she led me upstairs, talking about the house – the curve of the banister, the stained-glass window that had been stolen from the downstairs hallway one night, the way the landlord had replaced it with plain glass and what else could he do, really, but the house had lost some of its magic. When she opened her apartment door she pushed it too hard, slamming it into the foot of her bed, and the smell of incense rolled out and over us, as heavy as anything I'd ever inhaled in a West Bank head shop.

We already knew we were going to end up in that bed together, and it made us shy and awkward. She shrugged her jacket off and took mine from me, but instead of hanging them up the way I'd expected she tossed them on the floor in a corner, making it look like the freest and most normal thing in the world – the gesture we'd all make if only we could.

"I like to think this was the parlor," she said, nodding by way of explanation to the stained-glass panel that showed above a window shade. "All those ladies floating through in their beautiful dresses."

"All those ladies crippled by their corsets."

"You're being unromantic."

I couldn't help myself, though. I felt easy enough with her to argue. I felt uneasy enough to argue.

"A parlor would've been on the first floor."

"I like the idea. You don't want to take it too seriously."

The room was a fair size, whatever it had been, with a high ceiling. Probably a bedroom. Peg lit a stick of incense, then went into the bath-mat-sized kitchen and started clanging pans around and washing cups for coffee. I leaned against the open doorway, admiring the curve of her shoulder, the angle of her arm. She wasn't beautiful. I knew that and I didn't wish for her to be anything other than what she was. I felt easy with her. I liked the way she threw herself at things, the way she'd opened the door too fast so it slammed into the bed. I liked the way she banged around the kitchen. I liked that she held on to her idea of the parlor even though it made no sense. I liked that she argued with me. It let me know that when she did smile I could believe she meant it. I hate it when women pull their lips back and grimace because they think it's charming, or walk around with lukewarm I-won't-threaten-anyone smiles. Someone always pays a price for those smiles.

It went beyond attraction, what I felt for Peg.

She dried the cups she'd been washing – elegant, mismatched things marked with chips and hairline cracks – and set them next to the stove, where a pan of water was almost at a boil.

"It's instant," she said. "I ran out of the real stuff. Is instant okay?"

"Instant's fine."

It was fine – it was what I drank at home – but I'd have been happy to drink salted water with her.

She measured the powder and poured water on it, sending steam cascading upward. I loved the way her hand held a folded dish towel around the saucepan's handle, her wrist disappearing into the cuff of a flannel shirt. I loved the quart of milk she took out of the refrigerator. I was ridiculous and I knew it and I didn't care.

We carried our coffee to the apartment's two chairs, which faced each other in front of the window. She sat in a wooden armchair, leaving me a frou-frou, armless, ruffled thing that was too small for me but was upholstered in faded purple velvet and made me feel like I'd fallen in with displaced royalty. Peg was someone who gathered up whatever she found and made a home out of it, and I loved that too. All I'd made for myself was a place to camp, and until now I'd taken a kind of pride in not wanting more than that, but sitting in Peg's uneasy velvet chair I understood for the first time that I could allow myself something more – that I was hungry for something more.

Between us sat a round wooden table, a small, Victorian-looking thing that balanced unevenly on a single stem and splayed feet. I set my cup down and it weighted the table toward me, pulling the tide of coffee to the landward side of my cup. I picked the cup up and sipped coffee off the top. It tasted of incense, as if I'd sipped the heavy air of the room. I was having trouble, sitting that close to her bed, thinking of a single topic that two human beings could talk about, and I took another sip of incense-flavored coffee to fill the time. She stared into her own cup and I wondered if it would be okay to simply reach across the table and touch her. Her shoulder was round and full and calling to me. I didn't reach for her, though. It was too important that I get this right.

I set my cup on the table, rocking everything back to my side. I had a half-formed thought that we should talk about ex-lovers, moving through our histories until we'd each summed up the most recent one and said how much we'd been hurt by the breakup, after which we'd be so overcome with sympathy that our chairs would tip us gracefully in the direction of the bed. Before I figured out how to bring up either her exes or mine, though, she took refuge in the topic we'd done so well with before: family.

"You have any brothers or sisters?" she asked.

I was disappointed. I was relieved. I was still thinking we had to find a topic related to the bed.

"Not a one," I said. "You?"

At which point I remembered her father being tied to his job by children, plural, but if she remembered having mentioned that she didn't let it show.

"Sisters. Two of 'em. Younger."

I smiled as if this meant something special to me.

"Much younger, actually. I feel like I'm halfway their mother. We were—" She made a gesture with her hands that worked like a shrug. "By the time they were old enough to know what was going on, my father was sick, my mother'd given up the mommy routine. Things pretty well fell apart at home. And there I was, most of the responsibility and none of the power. I can't tell you how much fun it was."

She pushed herself up, crossed the room and lit a stick of incense, holding me suspended in the middle of the family collapse.

"I don't mean to whine. It's not like it was easy for my sisters either. I mean, they still call me as if I could fix stuff for them. Deena gets into trouble at school" – she raised a hand as if she was waiting to be called on – "she calls me. Mom has a fit about something, hey, maybe I could talk to her and that'll make it right. The time Jude broke her finger, my mother was I have no idea where, so guess who got to drive her to the emergency room. And guess who didn't have the insurance information. Guess who isn't her guardian. The thing is, whatever I do, it doesn't help. It's all still a mess. Nothing changes."

I was nodding a quiet beat, understanding that she was allowing me into something that mattered to her, understanding that if I could swim this river of anger and sadness with her it would carry us to the bed as surely as the ex-lovers would have.

That sounds like I didn't care how she felt, but I did. I cared about everything she wanted to tell me, but that didn't mean my thoughts were pure. She was still standing by the incense burner and I went to her, hesitated, put my arms around her, and she melted into me as if I were the source of all the comfort the world would ever offer her. Instead of pulling her toward the bed, though, I let her go and told her what I'd managed not to say about my own family. I told her about my father's drinking, and then about my mother's, although my mother's was more or less an afterthought since I'd had so many extra years to watch my father dance with the bottle. It had nothing to do with what Peg had just told me, but in the odd logic of the moment it also did. We came to each other with these histories clanking behind us, these tin cans tied to our tails. Talking about them did nothing to bring us together on that bed, though, and we sat down and were awkward again for a few seconds.

"It doesn't matter," I said, knowing it did. "I don't know why I brought it up."

Peg gave me the kind of look you give someone when you're sitting near the bed and working your way toward it.

"Tell me one good memory you have of them," she said.

It took me a minute. I was closer to the bad ones. They were more comfortable.

"We had this next-door neighbor," I said. "You know the type. Hates kids, ball lands in his yard he'd set his house on fire before he'd give it back. I'd leaned my bike on his fence and he came out and started yelling at me, and I mean he scared me – I was maybe seven, eight years old. You know, little. Anyway, my mother came out, slamming the screen against the side of the house, pointed a finger at him like she could shoot lightning out the end of it, and she yelled that he wasn't ever to talk to me, he wasn't to so much as look at me, I was her kid and if he had a problem with me he could damn well take it up with her."

I stopped talking for a minute, remembering the feel of my mother's arm pulling me tight against her and the safety I felt leaning there, as if nothing could ever hurt me again.

"It's funny, because when something happened the first thing she usually did was blame me."

Peg nodded, and waited in case I had something more to say.

"She was fierce," I said after a while.

"I like fierce women."

It sounded sexy the way she said it, and like a compliment to me somehow, which made us both grin and then get embarrassed so that we picked up our half-cold coffee and sipped at it, but then we set it aside and touched – hands, an elbow, a shoulder, a cheek – and moved to the bed, throwing all its velvety cushions on the floor in a scattering of peacock colors and India prints, and we began as ancient and natural and awkward a series of acts as the human race knows. Each time we unbuttoned, unzipped, untangled, we got embarrassed all over again, as if we'd forgotten each other's names, and each time that happened I thought maybe she wasn't ready, maybe I wasn't ready, maybe we were about to ruin everything, and then something would catch us again – a breath of air; a current; a gale – and I stopped thinking for another stretch of time and let the wind carry me.

I was half a second short of taking flight when the phone rang and I felt a shift in her attention. I dug my fingers into her shoulder.

"Let it ring."

I was panting. I was damn near begging. The truth was that I couldn't take flight with just anyone. It had been a while since I'd slept with anybody, and if I couldn't make it that night I didn't think I'd work up the courage to try with her again.

She came back to me, though, reinhabiting her hand until I flew, and I loved her in that moment in a way I'd never loved anyone before. In a way I never expect to love anyone again. The phone rang and rang, and I wrapped myself around her and laughed.

"Someone's persistent," I said, when I was ready to think about something more than the two of us.

She reacted. I couldn't have said how exactly, and I had no idea what it meant, but I could feel the sharpness of it.

"It doesn't matter," she said, and she pulled me back to her, closing the space I'd made when I started talking.

Much later – the damn phone was still ringing – I got out of bed to lift the receiver, hang it up, and take it back off the hook. I crawled into bed again, put my arms around Peg and felt her skin soft against my breasts. I kissed the curve where her neck met her shoulder. I was as pleased with myself as if I'd figured out a practical method of space travel.

. . .

We lay in the dark for some time before either of us felt the need to say much.

"I wondered how we'd get to this point," I said eventually.

"Hah, there's self-confidence for you. I wondered if."

I was getting all rosy again and I kissed her shoulder, not because I wanted to make love again right away but because it was a language we could speak now. She ran a hand over my hair, but partway through the gesture it changed and she palmed my skull as if she wanted to keep me from turning away.

"I have to tell you, I wasn't sure we should do this," she said. Her voice was sober and struck me as dangerous. "I'm still not sure."

My brain said, *It's too late*, but the words stayed shut up inside. I looked at her – round face, brown eyes, a thread of hair falling crossways over her forehead, all the bits and pieces exactly the same as they'd been before but all of them changed somehow, all the energy gone out of them.

She moved her hand off my skull and I felt as cold without it as if she'd left me bald.

"I owe you an explanation," she said.

"You do?"

"Of what's going on. You remember Megan."

More statement than question. Megan. Who the hell was Megan?

"From the Coffeehouse."

Right. The dance floor, with the couple I tried not to stare at doing dips and twirls beside us.

"Your ex?"

"She's not my ex. She's not *my* goddamn anything. I didn't go out with her long enough to make her my ex. I barely know the woman."

Her anger swept over us like a gust of wind, then it blew itself out, leaving us becalmed in an ocean of incense.

"Okay. Megan. Yeah, I remember her."

She rolled onto her back and said she was sorry. She didn't say what for but I took it to mean she wasn't mad at me and even though I'd sort of known that I still felt better. It hadn't been me who'd called Megan her ex. That had been someone else, and it had been insensitive as all hell.

"There's nothing to be sorry for," I said.

She got out of bed and lit a new stick of incense. She was looking for something to do with herself and I could see that, but what struck me was how easy she seemed, in the middle of her uneasiness, about walking around naked.

She came back to bed but didn't crawl in beside me. She wrapped herself in the bedspread and pulled her knees up to her chin.

"I'm not sure I'm—"

She gave that up as a bad start.

"Let me tell you the story, then you decide if you want to get into this mess."

She looked sober and alone and far more vulnerable wrapped in her India-print bedspread than she had naked. I would have touched her again but didn't feel I had the right anymore.

She looked away from me but kept talking.

"I went out with Megan exactly three times," she said. "Or not exactly. It was twice, because at the end of the second date I called it off. There was just something weird about it, something – I don't know. Off, somehow. Wrong."

She was still looking away from me, trying to fit words around what was wrong about it maybe, or else remembering things she didn't want to tell me.

A couple of days after she'd ended it, she said, Megan called her and wanted to talk. No, not *wanted* to talk but *needed* to talk; needed to not just talk but *meet* so they could talk, and Peg went.

"I had this kind of wounded animal thing about her, you know? I'd pull the thorn out of her paw and she'd go dancing on her way. And I was flattered, you know? I was fucking flattered. I was the person she'd turned to. I was – shit, I don't know what I was. I was a junior therapist is what I was, complete with the cereal box tops and the Dick Tracy decoder ring."

She pinched one finger, watching it intently, reminding me of someone working a toothpaste tube, trying to squeeze a leftover quarter-inch of toothpaste back inside. Then she caught herself and tucked her hands under the bedspread.

"Christ, they warn us about boundaries. About not playing therapist with our friends. Well, I'm here to testify, they're right."

What Megan needed to talk about, it turned out, was why Peg was the only person she'd ever be able to love and whether or not she'd kill herself if Peg wouldn't come back to her and why Peg should come back to keep them both from finding out. She didn't threaten it, exactly. She talked about killing herself as if it was something outside of her, like rain, like hail, like a couch someone had pushed out a third-floor window – something that might or might not land on her. They'd met in a late-night donut shop and they sat there for hours, with Megan talking about what Peg meant in her life and Peg explaining why one day some other woman would make Megan fifty times happier than she could.

"You should've seen me," Peg said. "I was so fuckin' patient with her I could just kick myself."

Her hands had worked their way back out of the bedspread and she was squeezing that toothpaste tube again.

"I mean, I was *good*, and I kept *thinking* how good I was. Sympathetic. Nonjudgmental. I remember telling her at one point that she had a lot to contribute to the world and it'd be too bad if that was lost, and then I thought, *Fuck, what do I say if she asks me* what *she has to contribute?* Because I couldn't think of a thing."

She curled her hands around each other to keep from pinching that finger.

"It must've been – I don't know, midnight, one a.m. Three. I don't know. It was late. There was some guy at the back table arguing with the air and this other kind of mossy-looking guy who hadn't washed his hair in six months and had a stack of books on the table, probably reading up on UFOs or something. So we were sitting in Losers' Alley, and I want to tell you, I felt like part of the freak show – two dykes talking about suicide and unrequited love. Right out of *The Well of Loneliness*, only the low-rent version."

We looked away from each other. The incense was rising in a double line, curling up from the glowing tip like two different predictions for our future – no telling what they were or which we should choose, but they clearly separated at the moment they left the tip: here is one possibility and over there another. Choose wisely. It wasn't yet midnight but it felt later, as if no one was left awake on our side of the planet, just the two of us, Peg wrapped in indigo and off-white and me with both pillows behind my head and the covers pulled up to my shoulders.

Peg finally left Megan sitting at the donut shop and drove home. It was so late that the lights at the intersections were flashing either red or yellow, stop or caution. She was grateful to have that part of her life behind her.

Except, of course, that it wasn't behind her, because Megan called, Megan sent letters, Megan followed her car. Peg couldn't even answer the phone like a normal person. If I wanted to reach her, I'd have to let it ring once, hang up, then call back.

"I came home last week and found all these chopped-up flowers in front of the door. I mean, not just chopped – *shredded*. I don't know what the hell it's supposed to mean. I don't even know how she did it. Chewed 'em. Ran 'em through the blender. I'm telling you, it's weird. It's scary."

I pictured Megan – I still thought of her as Peg's ex – and she was a flea. Small, with the unmuscled thinness of a woman who hadn't counted on her body for anything but looks – or sex, presumably – since she got out of grade school.

"So that's what you're getting into," Peg said. "I mean, I don't want to take things for granted – if you want to keep seeing me."

"I want to keep seeing you."

Her face didn't clear, and I don't suppose mine did either. We might as well have been declaring war on a larger, better armed country.

"I haven't gone out with anyone since this started," she said. "I have to tell you, I'm nervous about it."

I said all the right things. It would be fine. Megan was nothing to worry about. We'd get through it together. Words like a lullaby. Sleep, sleep, there are no monsters, sleep. The shades were down and we were cut off from the world, wrapped in lathe and plaster and stucco, in double layers of glass and drawn shades, in darkness and incense. It would all be all right. Everything would be all right.

In the morning, we walked to the store and bought eggs, milk, real coffee, the Sunday paper, a package of pineapple rolls, and we walked home through the cold with that romantic feeling you get when you're doing something you know you'll look back at later as an anniversary. Our first morning together. Our first groceries. Our first breakfast. They made us a couple. It had snowed the night before, just enough to resurface the snowbanks and leave a dusting on the sidewalks, and the sky was the brittle blue of a January cold spell. Sunlight bounced off the new snow, glittering and making Peg's eyes water so that she dabbed at them with the tips of her mittens to keep the tears from spilling over and freezing on her cheeks. I walked with my head bent forward and my eyes squinted against the glare.

"What do you think?" Peg asked. "Ten below?"

"Easily."

"You like winter?"

I had just shifted the groceries from one arm to the other so I could warm the frozen set of fingers in my pocket. We were almost at her corner and I was looking forward to wrapping both hands around a cup of brewed coffee.

"Grew up in Duluth. I've seen all the winter I'll ever need."

I turned toward her to smile, inviting her to agree so we'd have one more thing we shared. Instead of agreeing, though, she yanked on my arm, pulling me backward, almost making me drop the groceries. Before the corner of a building cut off my view, I caught a glimpse of Megan, planted in front of Peg's building and looking up at her window. Or I assumed it was Megan. In a Minnesota winter, you don't see actual people on the streets. You see clothing, layers and layers of it, moving from one place to another, waiting at bus stops, struggling into cars. This particular collection of clothes was small and seemed to contain a human, probably a female, presumably Megan.

"God damn her," Peg said, and then, "Don't stop. Don't look at her."

Megan was out of sight by this time. I couldn't have looked at her if I'd wanted to, but her image had burned itself into my memory, the knit cap that was pulled low on her forehead tipped back so that a small patch of face pointed at Peg's window like the dog in the RCA ad looking at the Victrola.

At the alley, Peg stopped pulling me and kicked the hard-packed snowbank.

"God damn her. That goddamn little shit-fuck shitfaced fuck."

She kicked the snowbank and combined *shit* and *fuck* a few more times.

I switched the groceries to my other arm and waited, feeling oversized and useless and cold. I seemed to be watching Peg from half a block away, observing that she was pitching a fit.

"You want to go in through the back?" I said finally.

"She'll see us."

I could have argued sight lines and probabilities with her, but I understood that they were beside the point. All that energy I loved in Peg, all that forward motion, was gone. If anyone was going to throw herself into this, it would have to be me, because Peg was going to stand there kicking the snowbank.

"I hate this," she said. "I hate what she's doing to me. I hate what she's turning me into."

She swiped at her eyes again.

"I'm going to go talk to her," I said.

She clutched the arm I'd wrapped around the groceries. "Don't do that."

I hesitated, not ready to give in, not ready to pull away.

"You'll make it worse."

"It's already worse."

We balanced there for a long, slow couple of seconds.

"We can't spend our lives hiding around corners."

"What're you going to do?"

"I don't know. Talk to her. Tell her to go fuck herself."

I handed Peg the grocery bag and she accepted it, neither one of us acknowledging that what we'd just done meant I had something more in mind than talking, although I did, I suppose.

When I got close enough to the corner to see around the building, Megan's arm was in the home stretch of hurling something at the window.

I yelled, "Hey, you," and started running. On the sidewalk, ice lay under the snow and my feet skated backward each time they pushed off so that I ran in slow motion, worried as much about falling as about catching her. Something splattered on the building – egg, I thought, and that connected in my mind with the eggs in our grocery bag. I had an incoherent sense that she'd just thrown our breakfast – the one we hadn't made yet; the one with brewed coffee that was going to make us a couple – all over the front of Peg's building, and I felt the kind of rage a baby must feel if you pop the bottle out of its mouth when it's just started to suck. I yelled all the way down the sidewalk and she turned and scuttled toward her car, her feet sliding as badly as mine were. I was close enough behind her to scale the snowbank and pound on her roof, kick her door, and then pound on the trunk as she pulled past, yelling the whole time, even after she'd skidded out of reach. If I'd thought about it, I could have tried the passenger door to see if it was locked, but that didn't come to mind until she'd fishtailed around the corner, when I also thought that I could have run to the driver's side and pulled her out.

I didn't stop to ask myself what I'd have done once she was out of the car, or I was in.

"We can't just hide from her," I said, while Peg fumbled her key into the downstairs lock. "It gives her all the power."

I was carrying a carton of eggs Megan had dropped in the snow when she ran. Who did that give power to? Had we stolen her eggs or was something of hers invading Peg's apartment? I flipped the carton open when we got upstairs. Four eggs were missing and one was smashed and leaking into its cardboard nest. It all seemed immensely sad and stupid and violent. I poured the broken egg down the drain, which left seven and a little spilled white, but that didn't lessen my sense that something had been damaged.

Since we had the groceries, we went ahead and made breakfast. Peg unpacked the bag and broke eggs into a bowl with enough force to crack skulls, using our eggs, not trusting Megan's. I tore the plastic film off the pineapple rolls. To not eat, we'd have had to tell each other that we weren't hungry anymore. We'd have had to admit that Megan had changed us, which of course she had. We went through the motions of eating but neither of us had much of an appetite.

We didn't talk about that, though. We talked about Megan and what she'd done, and how she'd done it, and why she'd done it, and what we could do about it. We circled through it and then back through it again in one of those over-amped states where it seemed like talking too loud and too fast might drive her out of our systems. It was Peg, finally, who said she couldn't stand to talk about Megan anymore and opened the Sunday paper, closing herself off from me as well as from Megan. I picked up a random section of newspaper and tried not to feel left out.

We didn't touch until later, when I said I should go home, and then we clutched at each other as if we were drowning and had decided to go down together.

As soon as I closed myself into my car, I couldn't remember why I'd thought I had to leave, but it was too late by then to go back.

At work on Monday, I carried Peg with me. And Megan. I don't know which one was the more powerful presence. I watched the traffic and the snowbanks and the buildings slip past that big windshield and replayed the image of myself pounding on Megan's car. I told myself I'd scared her. Hadn't she dropped her egg carton and fishtailed around the corner to get away from me?

I pulled up next to curbs where people were waiting. I opened the doors and they fed their money into the fare box. They said good morning and how's the driving and it's a cold one today, isn't it, and I said all the right things back to them. They pulled the cord and got off, and as soon as they were gone they might as well never have been there. If they'd all unpacked automatic weapons and attacked the Foshay Tower, I wouldn't have been able to pick one of them out of a lineup, although I could have identified the rust pattern on Megan's car, along with the boot-sized dent that I might have left by the door handle, although it might just as easily have been there when she parked outside Peg's building.

By the end of the day I knew I hadn't won my round with Megan, and I knew there was no way to reorganize the facts so I'd feel like I had. And I also knew – or thought I knew, or at least was afraid I knew – that I couldn't go through what had happened on Sunday morning over and over and still stay in love. Because love doesn't conquer all, and even then I had half guessed that. It does the best it can, but like most things in our atmosphere, it oxidizes. If it doesn't outright rust, some free radical comes along, makes a minute change in one lousy cell, and before you know it one of you is dead and where the hell does love go then? If I had to fight my way past Megan and a carton of eggs every weekend, if I had to either hide from her or pound on her car and wonder which of us had rattled the other one more, sooner or later I'd hate myself. I'd wait for Peg to shut herself off behind the newspaper and hate me, and maybe after a while she would. Maybe she'd have reason to. Maybe before she got a chance, I'd learn to hate her.

And so I did the most comfortable thing I could do: I hated Megan. For what she'd done. For what she would do. For what she had the power to make me and Peg do.

Still, I went back to Peg's place that night, and the night after that, until it became a pattern. I never once thought of not going back.

As I got used to Peg, I stopped being overwhelmed by the thought of her as a therapist. I noticed that she let the dishes pile up in her kitchen until she ran out of either plates or the space to stack them in, that if she turned the vacuum on and then off she thought the apartment was clean. Silly things. Human things. They didn't turn me away from her but they settled me into a way of seeing her that didn't ask her to be perfect. But the change was also because of Megan, and because of the fit Peg had pitched when she spotted her that first morning. I couldn't kid myself that Peg's life was any less screwed up than the average civilian's, and that wasn't entirely a bad thing.

We hadn't moved in together yet, although we might have if it hadn't been for Megan. Instead, I brought things to Peg's apartment and left them there: my bathrobe, whatever I was reading at the moment, a lamp that let us read in bed. And my coffee mug, because Peg's collection of flowered cups with their delicate handles and their saucers were elegant as all hell and I loved her for having them, but I wanted volume when I drank my coffee.

A couple of days after I brought the mug over, my attention wandered while I was washing dishes and I whacked it against the faucet.

Without meaning to, without knowing that I would, I wailed.

Peg came in from the other room to find me fishing fragments out of the dishwater and calling myself every kind of an idiot. She draped an arm across my shoulders.

"It's only a mug. Christ, I thought I'd find you bleeding on the floor. We'll get another one."

But there were rules in my life, and I couldn't just get another mug. I had to convince myself that I'd be more careful before I trusted myself with a new one. Or maybe I had to suffer a little. I don't know. It's not like these things make sense entirely. I threw out the soapy fragments, dislodging her arm from my shoulder, and tried to explain that I couldn't just buy one.

"That is so mean," she said. "It's punitive."

"Yeah, well, gravity can get nasty too."

I turned back to the dishes, leaving Peg to watch from one side, and I'd have turned my back on her altogether if I could have moved the sink. I had the feeling that if she watched me much longer she'd want to rearrange my molecules.

I cling hard to the parts of myself I like the least.

"Get out of here and let me finish the dishes before I break something else."

She hesitated, and for a minute I thought she'd argue, but instead she rubbed her hand across my back.

"You sure?"

"I'm fine. Get out of here."

She squeezed my shoulder and went, leaving me with the dishes, the sudsy water, a few fragments of mug that I hadn't found yet, and the thought that I was mean.

A couple of days later she came home with a mug as large as the one I'd broken and a deep, glowing blue.

"There," she said, folding my hands around it. "What're you going to do about that?"

It had a lovely feel in my hands.

I said, "I can't," but I didn't refuse to hold it.

She grinned as if I'd said thanks and she kissed the top of my head.

"Be nice to Marge for me, will you? I like her."

Mostly, though, in spite of the good moments, we lived through that winter like people under siege, clinging to each other, fighting, making up with an intensity that was out of all proportion to the fight we'd just had. We talked a lot about how to change the dynamic with Megan. We actually said that: *change the dynamic*. It started out as Peg's phrase, something she got from a textbook, or from one of her professors, but we both came around to using it. We forgot how absurd it was. Something about its dryness, its distance from actual human speech, made us think we really could change something and that the way to do it was out there somewhere.

On a good day it was out there. On a bad day there was no way – not as long as Megan knew how to find us. We talked about hanging on until Peg graduated, then changing our names and disappearing. We'd move to San Francisco, to Maine, to Indianapolis if we had to. We'd go into our own private witness protection program. We never did solve the problem of how Peg would use her degree if she couldn't use her name, but we gnawed away at the smaller problems as steadily as if the idea was practical.

Her main worry was staying in touch with her family, and the first time she talked about it I said of course she'd be able to stay in touch – Megan wasn't James Bond, for god's sake. She couldn't bug the phone or intercept the mail to find us. She wouldn't break into Peg's mother's house to steal her address book.

"You don't understand," Peg said.

She had that closed-off-behind-the-newspaper look about her, although the newspaper was nowhere in sight.

"So tell me."

She made an exasperated noise. We were at her place, me in the wooden armchair and her sitting cross-legged on the bed, stiff-backed and angry. For a few seconds I thought she wasn't going to answer, that whatever I was missing was either too complicated or too obvious.

"What if she finds Jude and starts asking where I am? Deena'd bite her head off, but Jude's—"

She shrugged. *Softer*, I supplied silently.

"So you warn her. You tell her not to tell anyone."

"I don't want Megan dragging the kids into this."

I gave up after that and let her supply both sides of the argument. It was easier on both of us.

I'm not sure who started the jokes about killing Megan, but they helped, in a bitter sort of way. They didn't make us feel better but they did let us laugh, which gave us the illusion that we felt better. It says a lot about the shape we were in, I suppose, that we thought they were funny.

Over time, the jokes changed shape. They had to or we'd have stopped laughing. I'd see Megan one day when I was working and just happen to run her over with thirty thousand pounds of bus. We'd let a contract on her. No, we'd let a pie contract – a hundred dollars to anyone who'd hit her in the face with a pie in public. We'd pay someone big and mean-looking to beat her up. We'd beat her up ourselves. And here we got serious. Would it change the dynamic – and there was that phrase again – if Megan had to pay a price for what she was doing to us? Was she doing it only because she could? By not beating her up, were we actually encouraging her?

We argued the question back and forth all winter, changing sides randomly, never both on the same side at the same time. One of us would argue that it was a solution out of a cop show or a western – you slug someone and then things get better. The cleansing flame of violence. It would bring us down to her level if we did that. The other one said it might work, and outside of the witness protection program it was the only solution we had. If restraining orders existed back then, we didn't know about them. The only people who talked about stalking were hunters. If we'd gone to the police, what would we have said? She called on the phone? She threw an egg at the house? Oh, hell yes, then, string her up.

We had a few friends who knew what we were going through, and Peg's family knew, but mostly we kept it to ourselves. When we had time on weekends, we went to Peg's mother's place just to spend a few hours where Megan had never been. It was a kind of vacation. We watched TV, cooked, ate, played with the cats, teased her sisters. Peg was close to her sisters in a way that fascinated me. I studied Peg and her sisters and thought, with a mixture of distance and hunger, that this was what sisters were like in real families. They bickered the way some people played board games or worked jigsaw puzzles, just to have something to do together. Peg saw it as her task in life to make them like school so she could drag them out of the world of time clocks and early pregnancies, and she refused to notice that learning didn't light them up the way it did her. She hounded them about homework, gave them books she thought they'd like even though we never saw evidence that they read anything more than they had to. If our lives had been anything like sane I might have told her to let it go since it wasn't helping, but it was all so utterly, stupidly normal that I looked forward to it. I told myself it was her way of encouraging them, of letting them know she cared. I told myself I didn't know the first thing about how normal families worked. I stroked whichever one of the cats was available and followed the flow of their squabbling until my muscles relaxed and I felt almost whole again, almost Meganless.

A couple of our friends had appointed themselves our bodyguards, but even with them we couldn't let our guard down. We went to the Coffeehouse one night and came out to three flat tires. Another time Megan followed us all into a restaurant and when the table next to ours emptied out she picked up her plate and moved in like a very small occupying army, watching us, listening to our conversation, and all we could think to do was shift our chairs so we faced away from her. We finished our food and left without ordering dessert. But even if the bodyguards could have kept her away, sooner or later they had to go home, and we had to go home, and it went back to being just us again – me and Peg. Me and Peg and Megan.

Peg came home from her internship to more shredded flowers – not by the downstairs door, where they'd been the first time, but in the hall outside her apartment, which meant not only that Megan had a thing about shredded flowers but also that she'd gotten past the downstairs lock. Peg and I developed permanent aches in our neck and shoulder muscles, and we spent hours trying to massage out the tension while the TV played.

Megan found my apartment too and left me a dead fish. Or parts of several dead fish – it was hard to tell. They were ugly, red-fleshed chunks, still wedged into their supermarket container and sitting outside my door. They smelled fresh, so I gave them to a neighbor for his cat. He told me later that they were so ugly the cat wouldn't eat them, and I was relieved. It made no sense, but I'd started to worry that Megan had poisoned them. Besides, the color made them look vaguely like human flesh.

A few weeks after that, someone built a fire on the sidewalk. I wasn't home when it happened – I heard about it from the neighbor. Then there was a fire in Peg's alley, a small one that did no damage. It was a damp spring, and it hadn't been set near any walls. We joined a small cluster of neighbors who were standing around the drenched remains and blaming neighborhood kids. We listened for a minute and turned away as if we had nothing to add.

In the upstairs hallway I put a hand on Peg's shoulder and she leaned against me and let me hold her as if we both thought I could protect her.

"She's just trying to freak us out," I said, my lips brushing the hair on top of her head, murmuring into it as if these were the sweetest words I knew. "The trick is not to let her."

She agreed, we wouldn't get freaked out, but somehow before bedtime we'd gotten into an argument about the witness protection program. I didn't understand what it would mean to move away from her family, she said.

"So shoot me, okay? What am I supposed to do, go back and grow up in a normal home?"

We were standing at opposite ends of her room, too pissed off to either sit down or stand next to each other.

"Use your imagination."

"I don't fuckin' have an imagination."

Which even then struck me as a strange thing to say. I felt an odd pride in how complete a denial it was, and how hard it would be to answer.

"You are the most frustrating—"

She'd brought her voice under control and sounded as if she was doing nothing more than describing what she saw in front of her, in the most unbiased possible way, and she walked past me into the kitchen to wash dishes as if I'd gone home, as if she'd forgotten me already. I grabbed my jacket and stormed out, slamming the door behind me.

I thought about driving home but instead walked aimlessly and fast, my head down, my hands in my pockets, replaying the argument, counting out the ways I'd been wronged and the reasons she was at least as frustrating as I was. After a while I came back to the idea of driving home because it seemed like the only way to dramatize how I felt: I'd go home and sleep in my own narrow bed, and I wouldn't call to tell her where I was. Tomorrow if she asked I'd explain that I hadn't thought she wanted me around.

I almost convinced myself it was true and at the same time I knew it wasn't. Both. Simultaneously.

What stopped me from getting into my car was the bareness of my apartment now that I was used to hers. If I couldn't make myself turn back for Peg herself, I could at least turn back to the home she'd made, with all its mismatched luxuries.

She must have heard me on the stairs, because she was standing by the window and waiting for me with her arms folded, watching while I didn't slam the door, and once I was inside she turned away. The idea gathered inside me that we'd have to split up, not because I wanted to but because she'd folded her arms and turned away from me, because she'd walled herself off, because something outside us both dictated that when these things happened relationships were over. But even with her arms folded like a barricade and her head turned aside, even then I wanted to run my hand down her neck until it rested on her shoulder. I wanted to press her against me until we were as perfect as we'd been at the start.

She turned toward me as if she'd been consulting with someone and had it all worked out now.

"Look, that was unfair."

I wasn't sure which piece of what I'd done she was analyzing and I waited, suspended and ready to argue.

"If I tell you I'm sorry, is that good enough?"

I nodded, afraid to do anything more. I wasn't clear about what started our arguments and I was even less sure about what it took to end them, but I was almost ready to apologize myself now that I wasn't being asked to.

"It's the stress," she said. "We're not ourselves."

I nodded: yes, stress. It was stress. I touched her shoulder, ready to pull away if she didn't soften, but she leaned her cheek down to rest it on my hand.

Love's such a strange thing. One minute the world's crashing down around your head, the next minute everything's fine. It was fine right then. We'd carved out a tiny cave in the flow of time and everything inside it was fine.

I hit my limit the night Megan threw shoes at Peg's window. Not because it was awful. For a second I thought she might break the glass, but they were toddlers' sneakers, probably from someone's garage sale – too small and too soft to break anything, and she hadn't thrown them hard anyway. Maybe it was because it was so stupid, or so strange. Maybe it was just because it came after the other things Megan had done. It was like knowing someone who'd once walked into your house and poured motor oil all over your living-room rug and then a week later you see her on the street and she's carrying a quart of 10W30.

You react.

You overreact.

It's natural.

Peg and I both ran to the window when the first shoe hit. Peg pulled the shade down and was all set to pretend we weren't home, hadn't just pulled the shade, didn't hear the thumps, and I was as angry at Peg as I was at Megan. I slammed out the door and down the stairs, and I chased Megan as far as the corner, yelling the whole way. I stopped there because she was in her car already and squealing the tires, but I'd have had to stop soon anyway. I was breathing hard, wheezing in air that was flavored by damp soil, new grass, the possibility of rain. I'd run half a short block from Peg's house – two-thirds if we're being generous – and already I felt like someone had clenched a fist under the spot where my ribs met, catching my lungs in their grip. I wasn't built for speed, and Megan was. And she would always be able to find a time when Peg and I were asleep, when we were watching TV, when we were wrapped around each other, although that didn't happen as often by then as it once had. She'd had an effect on us that way too.

I fumed my way up the stairs, still breathing hard, and slammed the door behind me.

"If you're going to hide from her, then hide from her," I said. I'd worked myself into a satisfying fury at Peg now that Megan was out of reach, and I felt like I'd latched on to the edge of some absolute truth. All I had to do was say the words loud enough and the rest of it would reveal itself. "Don't go to the window. Don't pull the shade while she's watching and pretend she'll think you're not home."

I was louder than I'd expected to be, and mean in my rightness, and the thing is, it felt wonderful. The world had never made as much sense to me as it did right then.

Peg looked at me blankly.

"It's not working." I meant what we were doing, but even more I meant what she was doing, although that might not have been at all clear. I wanted to go on and yell about everything she was doing to make it not work, because that had all been sharp-edged and certain when I was climbing the stairs, but the argument had gone shapeless on me.

"You done?" she said. Just that. Nothing more.

That was the first time I saw Peg get stingy with her anger, and it scared me in a way that her explosions never had. I said yes, I was done, making my concession into an extension of the fight.

"I know it's not working." Her voice was controlled and reasonable and insulting. "You want to pound on me for that or do you have a better idea?"

I turned away. I knew she was being unfair, and I wanted to throw that at her but couldn't get my head around how the unfairness worked. Again I thought about walking out and spending the night at my place but I wasn't sure what I'd have to convince her of in order to come back. Or convince myself of. Everything between us felt that fragile, that close to collapse.

Instead, I told her I was sorry, but even to my own ear I didn't sound sorry. She said "fine" though – grudgingly, the same way I'd apologized – and we retreated into the books we'd been reading before the first shoe hit.

We spent the rest of the evening staring into our books, turning pages as if each sound was a tiny insult, flattening our voices when we talked to remind each other how hurt we were. When we went to bed, we kept to our own sides and I lay in the dark thinking that it couldn't go on this way – that *we* couldn't go on this way. That I had to do something different.

The next day was a Sunday and Peg left for the library early to work on a paper. We said goodbye like acquaintances, and I didn't tell her I'd come to any sort of decision. I was deep in my own stinginess, and I was still angry for having apologized the night before when I didn't think I'd been at fault. Besides, I knew that if I told her I wanted to try something new she'd hesitate, and we'd have to discuss it, and the threat of another discussion weighed more heavily on me than anything else.

After Peg left I drove to a friend's house and borrowed her car, since Megan knew mine, and I parked in the lot behind Megan's building and waited for her to come out. Time passed. I had no reason to think that Megan would come outside, or would come out the back way instead of the front, so as much as I was waiting for Megan I was waiting for someone to come tell me I couldn't park there or for that morning's coffee to announce that it was time for me to leave. Sooner or later I'd go home and nothing would have happened but I would at least have tried, and maybe that would change the damned dynamic. I stared at the wooden back porches that ran the length of each floor, and at the stairs that connected them, and they struck me as an odd match for the brick of the building itself, like a skirt thrown on over a pair of jeans. More time passed. Even with the window open, the car was turning into a greenhouse. I was drowsy and began to wish I'd had more coffee, not so I'd stay awake but so I'd need to pee sooner.

I wished I'd told Peg I was coming here, and I got mad at her all over again for pulling the shade and setting off our fight.

Half an hour passed, or maybe it was an hour. I'd left my watch at Peg's and guessing the time was as hard as judging distance across water.

Eventually, Megan came down the stairs, wearing flip-flops and carrying a plastic garbage bag. The dumpster was at the far corner of the building, and she flapped toward it without noticing me. Her jeans had a hole in one knee and her T-shirt said "Celebrate!" She looked so normal that for long seconds I watched her as if she was a character in some movie, as if all this had to do with someone else, not with me.

Stepping out of the car felt as irrevocable as jumping out of a plane, and I seemed to be doing everything for the first time. I felt the ground under my feet with unusual clarity, each step a separate experience, the soles of my shoes telegraphing the details of pavement and pebbles, cracks and potholes, and they kept me from wondering what I was going to do when I caught up with her.

Which I did at the dumpster.

When I'd imagined this moment, I'd imagined that great American art form, the fair fight. Or fair except for the advantage my size gave me, which is another way of saying not fair at all. What I did, though, was slam into her just as she was turning back from the dumpster, pounding her against its metal side. She cried out, and she flailed at me, catching me on the breast and hurting me just enough to make me feel good about hitting her. It wasn't a fair fight. It wasn't much of a fight at all. I hit her, and I hit her some more, and it felt good. It felt great. And that's the thing about violence. For a few seconds, for a few minutes, as long as you're winning, it does feel great. And then it's over, and whatever you've done, it stays with you. Your body remembers it, and it reminds you, night after night: your hand connected with bone under the flesh and it felt like this; the sound when she hit the dumpster was like that; she had blood and dirt mixed together on the toe of her right foot, and somehow that small hurt seems sharper than the others. And it eats at you the same way that losing does.

When I backed away from Megan she was crying, and yelling that she'd burn my car, she'd burn my building, I'd see what she'd do. Then, with only the smallest shifting of gears, she yelled, "You hurt me," managing to sound surprised, as if I hadn't come there to do exactly that. As if she hadn't just threatened to do worse than that to me.

I'd turned my back on her by then – I was maybe a car's length away – and I swung back, taking a small step toward her, a gesture of a step, more threat than actual motion. It was a playground kind of moment – I was going to pound her until she yelled, "I give." Or maybe I was going to. I have no idea what I was going to do. My body was steering itself by then. I know I had a strange amount of faith in a formal surrender, and I still believed that what I was doing needed to be done.

She yelled again that I'd hurt her. You'd have thought some law of nature was supposed to keep that from happening. I'd almost worked myself up to the point of hitting her again – I was still high on adrenaline and self-justification – but what stopped me was that torn toe, that mix of blood and dirt. The strap of her flip-flop had pulled out of the sole, and the blood was welling up around the nail of her big toe.

A playground injury, but it was an injury I could see, a pain I could imagine. I couldn't know how badly I'd hurt any other part of her, but this much I understood.

I stalked back to my borrowed car and drove away, but instead of going back to Peg's I drove to my apartment. I told myself it was because of the car – my friend wouldn't be home for a while and I had to wait to return it, and besides Peg was at the library – but the truth was that I didn't want to see Peg.

So I went home. I ran a bath and I sat in it, staring at the taps and at the yellow wall behind them until the water grew cold. What I felt wasn't regret exactly, but it sure as hell wasn't victory. It was a blankness, an absence. I felt the water around my legs, and the line where my knees poked into the air. I lifted my splayed fingers out of the water and lowered them back in. I soaped the split skin of my knuckles. I didn't think, *I'm trying to wash this off*, but the thought was there anyway, communicating through muscle and nerve impulse instead of words in the brain.

Eventually the water got cold enough to drive me out of the tub. I got dressed. I brought my friend's car back and she wanted me to come in and tell her everything, as if I'd just starred in the latest episode of a soap opera. We were standing on either side of her front door. I held the screen open and felt the old-fashioned spring pull against me, wanting to close. She rested one hand on the inside door. I said I couldn't stay and looked over my shoulder as if whatever I had to do was just down the street, calling my name.

"Well, at least tell me what happened. Did she show?"

"I got tired of waiting. And I'd had too much coffee."

"I'll go with you next time. Anyone has to leave, the other one can stay."

I said that would be great and she gave me the kind of look you give people when there's a mismatch between what they're saying and the way they say it. She didn't ask about it, though. We just traded keys and I drove back to my apartment.

After all but living at Peg's place for months, I felt the bareness of mine – the narrow rollaway with its army blankets, the lone folding chair at my table. The only place to sit comfortably was the tub, and I'd already spent as much time there as I could in one day. So I swept. I dusted. I mopped. I drove to the store for a squeegee and washed the windows. The phone rang and I stopped to watch it but didn't answer.

When Peg showed up at my door, it was hours later and I'd pulled everything out of the cupboards – I didn't have much left by then – and was washing gummy rings off the shelves. She knocked, I opened the door, and I had to either tell her what I'd done or not tell her, but I wasn't prepared to do either, so I stared at her slack-jawed, and she stared at me. She'd seen my apartment before – we'd stopped off any number of times so I could pick up clean clothes, a book, my mail – so her staring wasn't shock over the way I lived, or had once lived.

She was still standing in the hall.

"Want to come in?" I said, as if she would have driven over for some other reason.

She said, "Ya," exaggerating the two-tone Scandinavian *ah* the way white Minnesotans do sometimes to make fun of themselves, although nothing about her said she was joking, and she came through the door, looking around for a hint about what to do with herself. I kept one hand on the door, holding it open as if I expected her to turn around and walk back out. After a second or two, I closed the door.

"Megan's dead," she said. She was whispering – a dry, rustling sound, as if she had no more breath than this inside her.

We stood in my bare apartment, and it was this that engraved itself on my mind – the comfortless room I had to offer her. Some long-buried part of myself rose to the surface and wanted to offer her a soft chair, a cup of something hot, a kleenex, but nothing I owned offered comfort. It was all hard surfaces and squares torn from a roll of toilet paper. She sat on my lone chair and I sat on the floor facing her, my shoulder against the wall and my back touching the bucket and mop that I hadn't gotten around to putting away yet. A small, cold word formed in my head: *good*. No emphasis, no triumph, just that flat bit of punctuation marking an end, and all around it lay the wordless knowledge that there was nothing good about it.

"Outside the house," she whispered.

I nodded.

"Where it happened. Outside my house."

I nodded again – yes, I understood.

"I didn't know where else to go."

She didn't ask what I was doing at my apartment, where I'd spent so little time in the last half year, and that seemed to mark how strange the conversation was. I pulled myself off the floor so I could stand behind her and put my hands on her shoulders.

"I'm glad you came here."

She nodded. It felt all wrong – me standing behind her, my hands on her shoulders, her muscles not moving to welcome my touch.

"Sit with me," I said.

I gestured to the bed, and we sat side by side on its edge, but that felt wrong too. If I could have burst into tears and thrown myself in her lap I'd have done it, but I had no tears to offer. I couldn't even put an arm around her – that would have been worse than not touching.

"They said she set herself on fire," she whispered.

"Who said?"

She stared at the clean boards of my floor for a while before she answered.

"Patty and Dan."

Her neighbors from the one-bedroom downstairs. I knew them to say hello to, which was about as well as she did.

"Poured gasoline over herself. From one of those red cans."

There was a precision about this. We weren't going to rest until we'd gone through every detail. She was still whispering, dragging what she'd been told like a deer carcass across dry earth and gravel, resting between each burst of pulling.

"Patty said – Patty said she screamed for me."

"Jesus."

"I wasn't home."

She was still whispering.

"She never knew."

She stared at the boards. I stared at the boards.

"I wouldn't have gone down anyway. I wouldn't have gone to the window. I wouldn't even have known."

The grain in the boards resolved itself into patterns – the currents of a river, an almost-face where the edge of a board was nicked. She would have known, I thought. She would have heard. There must have been screaming. And she would have gone to the window. She always did go to the window.

A small part of me was still mad about that but it didn't carry much weight right then.

"Even if I had known."

A long wait.

"I wouldn't have gone down there."

A wait.

"What if she'd thrown it over me too? What if she'd burned us both?"

"She could have," I said. "She could've done that."

"She could have."

We sat.

"I'm glad you weren't there."

"I closed the shades. So I won't have to look out."

"You should stay here."

"She's dead."

"I know."

"She won't bother us anymore."

"I know."

We stared at the floor. I wondered whether Megan was still wearing her flip-flops when she lit the match. I imagined that the pain would be worse if you were barefoot, or if you had nothing but rubber soles under your feet. I knew that made no sense but I believed it anyway.

"Jesus," I said again.

"Jesus," she echoed.

Another long wait. I wondered whether her flip-flops had been too badly torn for her to push the strap back into the hole and wear them. It seemed important to know that. It really seemed to matter.

"Her real name," Peg said. "I don't think I ever told you this. Her real name was Dorothy. Dorothy Celeste Theriault."

Of course. Every tenth lesbian had changed her name back then, trying to shake herself loose from some piece of the past and turn herself into the person she'd rather be. The only surprise was that she hadn't called herself Sunbird or Snowstorm or Big Damn Oak Tree. That was the more usual range.

"Why *Megan*?" I asked after a while.

For the first time in what seemed like ages, Peg swung around and looked at me.

"She said it meant 'little strong one'."

She laughed, and even at a whisper it had a wild edge to it, as if it might somersault up the scale any second, landing out of control on the high notes.

"I don't know if that's from any actual language on this planet, mind you. It could be the long-lost language of the Amazons, which only she knew."

"Atlantis. The secret language of the matriarchs of Atlantis."

"Ah, fuck," she said.

"She got the last word in, didn't she?"

We spent that night wedged into my narrow bed, sleeping on our sides and rolling over in tandem. All night long, I woke from one shallow pocket of sleep or another, convinced there'd been no interval between one stretch of lying awake and the next. I tried not to think about the things that can happen to human flesh. I remembered the sound Megan made when I banged her against the dumpster, and the feel of a human body compressing against my knuckles. I thought about fire, about napalm, about melting rubber flip-flops. I thought about the Wicked Witch of the West and pictured Megan shriveling and crackling out of existence, screaming not in anger but in pain, and because it was the middle of the night the image wasn't ridiculous but horrifying. The orange glow of the streetlight seeped in past the shades, and anytime I managed to bend my mind away from burning it bent me right back.

I got up before the alarm, grateful to put the night behind me, and I dressed in the bathroom, but Peg woke while I was dropping my keys and change into my pocket. She called to me, still using that whispery voice, and I couldn't tell if it was out of a hazy sense that talking out loud would wake somebody up or if she'd never talk in a normal voice again.

I squatted down beside her.

"There's an extra key in the pen cup. By the phone."

She whispered thanks.

"Just dump the whole mess out. It's probably sunk to the bottom by now."

She whispered that she'd find it.

"You'll be okay?"

She nodded, her chin furrowing the pillow.

"I could call in today."

"I'll be okay."

It was the most chilling thing I'd ever experienced, that whisper in the orange-flavored darkness. I kissed her forehead and she didn't pull away. Her flesh didn't burn my lips on contact.

"I love you," I said, and she whispered that she loved me too, and still I didn't stand up. I was waiting to be swept up by some tidal wave of emotion that would clear everything else away, but it didn't come. My toes crimped, my leg muscles ached, and that was all.

"Go to work," she whispered.

I kissed her again and left.

I was on split shifts in those days, working both rush hours, and normally I went home and caught a nap in between, but I didn't that day. I was afraid to sleep, afraid to lie down, afraid of my bare apartment and even more afraid of Peg's lush one. I rode the bus to the Southdale mall and walked from store to store, fascinated by the obscenity of it all. I stared at comforters and couches, at bathrobes, at beds so advanced that they had to be called sleep systems, at sheer curtains and swag curtains and drapes and valances, at all the soft, expensive stuff that padded the cells of our lives. I couldn't have said what the truth was, but I would have sworn that these things existed only to hide it from us, and us from it. We should all live with bare walls, with hard floors, with stone, with ice. With rollaway beds, if we weren't strong enough to sleep on the floor. In the end, we died anyway. We died horribly. The sleep systems and the robes and the curtains didn't help.

I rode the bus back into the city and sat in a Vietnamese restaurant, but when my food came I looked at it and saw, instead of the meat I was used to eating, pieces of a bird that had once been alive, shellacked in its death with a translucent sauce. I ate the rice and picked out a few pieces of cabbage, and I drank tea, not for its taste but for its caffeine. I didn't feel tired but I wasn't sure the signals in my body were registering anywhere, so I had no way to measure how tired I might be. I stared out at the street and waited until I could go back to work.

The waitress stopped at my table. She was a small woman, no bigger than Megan had been, and in her early twenties, with a Vietnamese accent and an American way of carrying herself. She looked at my uneaten food and asked if everything was okay.

"It's fine," I said.

I had an impulse to try and explain – the cooked bird, the seared human, how odd it was that we all had this need to eat, but it would come out, I knew, sounding crazy.

"You don't eat," she said.

And for a second I thought it might all spill out anyway, more of my reasons than she ever wanted to hear.

"I know," I said. "It was my mistake."

My voice came out not quite as a whisper but softer than I expected.

I got through the second half of my shift. From out near the VA Hospital all the way to 26th Street, a man sat behind me arguing with the air. I thought about the man Peg had seen at the donut shop the night Megan talked to her about suicide. I thought how odd it was that someone like Megan shouldn't be visibly crazy while this poor guy was buggy enough to clear all the seats in a half-circle around him but was still alive.

When I got home, Peg was there. She'd brought some clothes over, and some of the food from her refrigerator.

"I kind of moved in," she said.

She had her voice back.

"That's good."

"You don't mind?"

I shook my head.

"I couldn't face being alone right now."

She looked at the floor as if I'd reminded her of something embarrassing.

"It's very clean," I said, nodding at the floor. "I mopped yesterday."

She tried to smile, and if she didn't quite manage it at least I recognized what she was reaching for. We were standing in the middle of my room, not sure what to do with ourselves. If we both sat on the bed, it would be like yesterday. If one of us sat at the table, the other one would have to sit on the floor or perch on the bed, on the far side of the room.

"We should bring over a chair," I said.

She turned to look at the table as if she could have managed not to notice its lone chair.

"And maybe the mattress. We could lay it on the floor and fold my bed up."

We hadn't talked about moving in together, but we'd agreed to as surely as if Megan had burned Peg's place to the ground.

"I don't want us to take this on as if it was our fault," she said. "This was a choice she made. We didn't make it for her."

There was an odd formality to the way she said this, and that felt comforting. She was the expert. This was her professional opinion. We were still standing, hands in our pockets, not sure where else to put them.

"I went over there," I said.

I'd looked away from her to say this but the jerk of her head drew my eyes back to her.

"What's it look like?"

I shook my head blankly.

"I went in the back," she said. "The shades are down. I was afraid to look out."

At that moment, if I had driven past the front of Peg's house I'd have described it for her and let her think that had been what I meant. If I'd even been able to guess, I might have pawned a description off on her. I flailed around for anything I could tell her other than what I meant, but all I knew was this one thing.

"Not your place," I said. "Megan's. Yesterday."

"Before she—?"

I nodded.

The muscles of her face rearranged themselves, working to assemble the information she now had into a new pattern.

"Before—?" she said.

"I beat the shit out of her."

She nodded, not giving her approval, just keeping track of the way the pattern was changing. I registered the exaggeration in what I'd said but couldn't decide if I was bragging or making sure I took on enough blame.

"Actually, it wasn't a beat-the-shit-out-of-her kind of thing. I did hit her, though."

Which was understating it, and I felt bad about that too.

"Before—" Peg said.

"Before."

As if I could have done it afterward.

"Did she seem—"

"I don't know. She seemed normal. You know. Surprised I'd be mad at her."

She scuffed her toe along my very clean floor.

"That's why she did it, though. I closed off the – you know. The door. I closed the door."

Her face had stopped processing and gone blank. I wasn't making sense. I walked to the window and looked at the street two stories below – the sidewalks, the parked cars. Nothing was moving. It was surprisingly easy to get lost in all that quietness.

"I told her I'd do it again if she bothered you."

Had I told her that? Did it matter if I hadn't? I was talking to the glass of the window but was sharply conscious of Peg behind me. Inside my head I heard the words, *All I did was what we talked about*, and I wanted more than anything else I could think of to say them to Peg. Whether they were an accusation or a plea or just a statement of fact I didn't know. I wouldn't have known until I heard the sound they made in the air. Maybe they were all of those. I rested my forehead on the glass and let the words turn to stone. Peg came up behind me and put a hand on my hip, her arm curving around my waist. For a while we just stood there, watching the parked cars. A piece of paper blew down the street, got caught behind a pickup's tire and stopped there. My street was bare of trees, flowers, grass, anything other than trash and clouds to mark the motion of air.

"We should move," I said. "Someplace we don't have any history."

"Not till I graduate."

It took me a minute to understand what she was thinking – the witness protection program. She hadn't taken in that life had changed. While I worked my way toward that, we stared out at the street.

"Another apartment," I said. "A place to start over."

She nodded.

We could have managed in my place – we'd been all but living together in hers, which was no bigger – but I'd already put my stamp on it, and I couldn't live like that anymore. And Megan had been there, leaving fish outside my door, lighting a fire on the sidewalk. When we packed, I wanted to leave her behind. We'd move someplace new and be the people we would have been if we'd started out clean, with no Megan in our lives.

"I never thought she'd do something like that," I said.

Peg pulled me a fraction of an inch closer.

"You had no way to know."

I nodded as if I believed her, but all the information had been right in front of me. Hadn't Megan told Peg? Hadn't Peg told me? Did I need someone to write it on my arm? Peg's hand rested on my hip, and her touch radiated outward along the nerves, making me lean into her, my body believing love was possible even while my mind turned away from its cost.

"If I'd known—" I said.

I watched the paper flap against the wheel of the pickup and then lie flat.

"I don't know if I'd have done it differently."

I pulled away as I said this, partly to see her face but partly, I think, so she wouldn't be able to pull away from me.

"You would have," she said.

"Yesterday, maybe. I don't know about another time."

"Neither of us knows what we'd have done."

I had my shoulder to the window frame and was watching her: round face, straight hair, the small nose where her voice was trapped. In that same cold and distant part of myself where I thought I might eventually have pounded Megan even if I had known what she'd do, I understood that Peg didn't believe that and never would. When she found a way to live with what had happened – and already I was sure she would – it would rest on her believing that I couldn't have known, that if I had known it would all have turned out differently. I'm not sure how I felt about that. I'm not sure I felt anything at all. It was simply true, the way a field or a tree or a parked car is true. How could I not have noticed it before? This was a weight I was going to carry alone, and I felt oddly peaceful about that. Megan's death, Peg's belief, the knowledge that she forgave me but had no idea what she was forgiving – I could carry all of that. I could protect her. She would never have to know that I was protecting her.

When we finally moved Peg's stuff out of her apartment, we went in and out through the back, leaving the shades down, and at the end of the alley we took a left so we wouldn't have to drive past the front of the house, even though there'd been time for the grass to grow back, for someone to come and scrub away whatever traces Megan had left behind. There've been moments when I wish I had looked, just to keep myself from trying to picture it later.

The apartment we moved into was a one-bedroom – modern and charmless and cheaper than what we'd been paying for our two places. We made my rollaway into a couch and Peg covered it with a garage-sale bedspread and all her cushions. We set the splay-footed table in front of it and nudged her armless velvet chair close to them, trying to make it all feel welcoming, but the place never had the comfort of her old apartment. Not even Peg could imagine it had once been a parlor. Still, we lived in it, and most of the time we weren't actively unhappy there. What we were was careful, as if the wrong word would shatter us. We stopped having fights – both the kind that brought us to our feet and the mean, stingy kind that, as I thought of it, had killed Megan. In their absence I felt, sometimes, as if we'd already left each other. I'd look at Peg and think that what we used to have was lost forever.

She never burned incense again. Not there, and not later, when we bought the house. I never asked why, and she never asked why I'd stopped eating meat.

Sometimes, though, at night, after I'd jerked awake and had to convince myself, first brain and then body, that I'd been dreaming, I would prop myself up and watch Peg breathe. It would take a while for the adrenaline surge to fall back, and I had time to wonder who I'd have been by then if we hadn't met, and who she'd have been, and whether Megan would ever have left her alone. I felt a weight, yes, and a loss, and I'd have given a lot to be rid of the dreams, but I never did wish myself back to innocence.

It's only now, when Peg's gone, that I've begun to wonder if there wasn't some piece of what happened that she kept from me. Sometimes I hope not, as if by imagining it that way I could keep her from having carried that weight. But sometimes I like to think there was something, and the thought that even now I don't know what it was, or even if it was, is like her hand resting on my hip, still sparking a response that runs from backbone to belly to thigh, my body still leaning into the emptiness and ready, even now, at any cost, to love her.

2

I DON'T want to romanticize what Peg and I had. There were things I could have wished for in our relationship, and more than one time when I went ahead and wished for them. I still believed in perfect relationships, and I compared what we had to what I thought dropped effortlessly into other people's lives, so whenever we failed to meet that standard I was sure we'd done something wrong, or in some essential way *were* wrong. I don't think that way anymore. We had what we had. Every time I turn around I find some new way that I miss it.

Most couples start fighting after they move in together, but we were too shell-shocked for that. We couldn't afford it. It wasn't until after Peg graduated, until she found a job and we bought the house, that the need to fight caught up with us, but once it did it behaved like the IRS, or a credit card company. The original payment wasn't enough. We owed interest. We owed a penalty on top of that. I'm not sure why we chose that time exactly. Maybe as long as Peg was in school we could believe that things would change once our real lives began. Maybe it took that long for us to feel safe enough. Maybe moving into the house reminded us of how much we missed each other, and – in the common insanity of the human species – instead of getting closer we turned on each other.

We started with the usual stuff. I walked in the door and found Peg's winter jacket on the floor and it didn't charm me the way it had that first night. Or I found a half-empty cup of coffee stranded on the bathtub rim. Or else it was money. Not the national debt – we were both working and we'd bought a house we could afford; it wasn't like we had to watch every cent. Still, she spent money in a way that scared me, buying new shoes when the old ones were still good, or a sweater when she didn't have enough room for the clothes she already owned. She never ran us into debt, but to me it felt out of control, unnecessary, and it was easy to draw a straight line from the small things she actually did spend money on to huge ones she might buy that would sink us. So the things that upset me were either things that hadn't happened yet or things that shouldn't have mattered, and I knew that, mostly, but before long I was telling myself that she knew they drove me nuts and if she kept doing them it meant she didn't care how I felt. And that was all it took, that one thought, and suddenly we were fighting about the relationship instead of the coffee cup or the shoes or the money.

And sex. We fought about sex. Or we didn't fight about sex but it was part of our fights anyway. I couldn't get there anymore, and I was sure she had something to do with that. Which I tried to explain to her exactly once, when we were still lying in bed, jangled and disappointed. I never did fake it with Peg, although I was tempted sometimes, more out of embarrassment than anything else. But if I ever crossed that line I was sure there'd be no way back, so she was feeling what had happened – or what hadn't happened – as sharply as I was, and I was lying on my pillow telling myself that when she touched me she wasn't really *in* the touch anymore because if she had been I would have flown with her, and so I owed it to us both to say so.

"About what happened," I said.

Already I could hear it going wrong.

"These last couple of times—"

It was wrong. I knew that and I went ahead and said it anyway because that's what I do sometimes. It makes no sense and I just go ahead and say it.

"It just feels like you're not really *there* when you, you know."

That was as close as I could get. Whatever freedoms the sixties had given me, that was as close as I could make myself go.

Peg, unfortunately, knew exactly what I meant.

"Oh, I'm *there* all right. I'm as *there* as I ever was. I can't get any *there*r, so don't try to make this into my little problem."

And she got out of bed and marched off to the shower, leaving me alone with my fingers, which turned out not to have any *there*ness to them either.

I lay in bed and listened to the water pound down on her, and I knew I should get out of bed and apologize, partly because I'd been wrong and partly because it would make life easier, but I didn't like the first reason and the second one was sleazy, and even though I didn't know where a phony apology would lead I knew I wouldn't like going there.

Peg drew away from me. Or I thought she drew away. For all I know I pulled away first, but I was sure it was her. Why wouldn't she draw away? I couldn't match her education. I wasn't good-looking. I was no fun in bed anymore. I wasn't even nice, and I knew that, but knowing only made me pissier. I'd have pulled away from me too if I'd known a way. We were distant with each other, and flat. It seemed to me that Peg's clients were the ones who got to see the real Peg, the intensely present Peg I'd fallen in love with, and for the first time since I'd known her I felt jealous: of her clients; of the more interesting, better educated, better-looking woman she'd leave me for eventually; of Peg herself, because those possibilities were open to her when they weren't to me.

So I started looking around, just to see what would be left in my life once Peg was gone, and I could always spot someone less complicated than Peg, someone more like me, someone who was just plain available. And in case I was in danger of forgetting them, I rehearsed all the things I wasn't getting from Peg anymore. Before I met her, what I wasn't getting had always been due north on the compass of my relationships, and I took an odd comfort in coming back to that old, familiar unhappiness, that one point in the universe I could count on finding. I measured and remeasured the distances that had opened up between us, checking to see if they'd grown, and they always had. We couldn't even talk about not arguing without turning it into an argument.

I was half convinced that Peg knew a way for us to break out of our mean inward spiral and that she was keeping it to herself, but being a therapist isn't like that and even then I knew it. You can back away from other people's lives and see what the people living them can't, but that doesn't mean you can do it for yourself. It doesn't grant you perfect pitch, or the ability to tap dance, or a gift for rising above your own mess.

I don't know if we'd have stayed together if Deena hadn't had a baby just then, although I'm not sure I can explain why that changed us. Maybe only because it gave us something to think about that was outside ourselves.

Deena was seventeen when the baby was born, and that by only a few weeks. She was also extremely single, which was just as well given the boys she fell for. No one was even pretending to be happy for her.

Rose – Peg's mother – called us from the hospital.

"A healthy baby girl," she told me, deadpan. "A miracle child. The doctors say she's ten years premature."

I laughed in spite of myself. It was hard not to with Rose.

We drove downtown after Peg got off work. We weren't arguing, but I'd straightened the house up after work and I could have recited the entire list of things Peg had left in strange places because she didn't care how I felt. The only reason I didn't was the fear that Peg would find something that was my fault and there we'd be again. So I sulked, waiting for her to notice how unhappy I was and change her entire way of being in the world.

I parked the car in a ramp, and instead of waiting while Peg dug our presents out of the back seat I turned away from her and walked to the front bumper, looking over a cement wall at a pebbled roof as if it was the most interesting thing I'd seen all day. It was late August, and sometime during the night the wind had shifted so that it came to us straight off the Canadian plains, ending a crushing spell of heat. That sort of shift usually made me feel like life was starting all over again, but it didn't right then. I noticed it and felt nothing. I heard Peg rattling the plastic bag behind me and kept myself from turning, withholding that small thing from her for no better reason than to show her that I could, to remind her how unhappy we were, just in case she'd forgotten. Or maybe I did it to make myself feel worse when she didn't notice me withholding it. I can't explain this so that it makes any sense. It was what I did. It was deeply and quietly insane.

Peg closed the car door, and I had to either turn or admit to what I was doing and open up the argument again.

I turned.

"I'll stop being mad if you will," she said.

We'd reached a point where she didn't have to ask if I was mad and the why of it barely mattered.

I nodded. One part of me didn't want to let go of being the injured party and the rest wouldn't admit that I'd been mad to start with, so I didn't trust my voice to sound gracious about this. If some genie had offered me happiness right then I think I'd have turned it down for the brooding pleasure of holding on to my grievance.

"Truce?" she said. "Peace?"

I'd left the cement wall and was standing at the rear bumper with her, and she swung the plastic bag into my legs as if she planned to whack me into a truce. She was filled with that energy I'd fallen in love with, as if she could open a tap and then demand that I come back.

"C'mon, damn it, sound happy about this. Say 'peace.'"

I said, "Peace." It was easier when we could treat it as a joke. It kept us from wondering who'd lost.

"We can afford it," she said. "My mother's going to be unhappy enough for everyone."

She was right about her mother. We might as well have walked into a wake. Rose and Peg's sisters were all staring off in different directions, as if each of them could make the other two go away. Jude was tilting one of those drugstore toy-aisle games, trying to settle its tiny metal balls into pockmarks that were too shallow to hold them. If Deena was seventeen, that would've made Jude close to fifteen, but she looked younger right then, like a sixth-grader sitting in a high-school class and trying not to draw anyone's attention. Deena was watching TV with the baby asleep on her lap, and Rose was staring out the window, looking grim.

Peg dumped our bag on the bed.

"Brought you some baby stuff," she said.

Her voice was too loud against all that silence, working too hard to be happy. I still thought of Peg as someone who understood people – all people, at all times – and who knew how to be with them, but she hit the kind of false note right then that I might have.

Deena reached into the bag and pulled out a tiny zippered suit – yellow, with multicolored trim.

Jude said, "Cu-ute," setting her game down and stretching the sound out so she cooed the word. Jude was the family's good girl – the conventional kid, the boring kid, the kid who wanted a fifties sitcom family instead of the odd, bristly assortment she'd been landed with – and I was grateful to her for all of that right then.

"I like the piping," Deena said.

"It's got plumbing?" Rose said. "Wish they'd had that when you were little."

"Piping, Mom. *Pi*ping. This stuff." She held the suit out, trimmed edge forward. "Jeez. Don't show your ignorance."

"Whose kid is this?" Rose asked the world at large. "She never heard of a joke."

Deena ignored her and dug in the bag again, bringing out pacifiers, a stuffed caterpillar that played a lullaby, a package of diapers and one of wipes, a pack of bibs, a rattle. Peg and I half sat against the windowsill to watch, as fascinated as if we hadn't just picked it all out and paid for it.

"You could have my chair," Jude said.

In tandem, we said we were fine.

It was odd how when Peg and I were with other people we could play the couple for them, giving ourselves a few moments when we really were fine, when we didn't snipe, didn't argue, just made ourselves into the people we wanted them to think we were.

"You guys went all out on the wrapping paper," Deena said, fingering the Target bag, making the plastic crackle.

"The word you're looking for is 'thanks'," Rose said. Another joke. You could have sliced a finger open on Rose's jokes.

Peg overlapped Rose, saying, "Treat that with respect, it was expensive," which let Deena ignore Rose as if she hadn't heard her. She unwrapped a corner of the baby's blanket, held the rattle in the baby's hand and waved it back and forth, putting on a baby voice to say, "Thank you so much. You're my favorite aunts."

"Oh, thanks," Jude said.

"Except my aunt Hey Jude, who I just love."

Jude hated being called that, hated anyone humming the tune.

"Yeah, right," she said.

Deena kept the baby voice to say, "All right, forget it, then. I don't love my aunt Hey Jude."

"You are so rude," Rose said, relieving me of the itch to giggle.

Deena picked the cash register receipt off the bed – it had fallen out with the baby suit.

"So how much do you think I'm worth?"

"Less than that," Peg said, "but there's the baby to think of."

Deena laughed, but she looked at the receipt long enough to check the amount.

Even with a hospital-issue gown hanging on her like an overwashed pillowcase, Deena was the beauty of the family – thick hair, long eyelashes, the full-scale conviction that she was beautiful. She wasn't quite, but she could make you think she was. What did it was that same energy I'd fallen for in Peg, but with Deena you had the feeling that it could shoot her off in any direction, or in all of them at once. It was attractive, but if you had any sense you kept your distance.

"Here, don't be selfish," Peg said. "Let me hold that baby."

Deena handed her over and Peg stood in the middle of the floor, talking about how tiny her hands were, how beautiful her face was, although she looked like every other squish-faced baby I'd ever seen.

When Peg ran out of parts to admire, Deena talked about all the things new mothers always tell people: the labor, the delivery, how when people told her it hurt she'd understood that they meant it but she hadn't understood how much they meant it.

"It makes me think maybe all that pain's there for a reason," Deena said. "Like because without it mothers might not appreciate their kids. Because people don't appreciate the stuff that comes easy."

She talked on, a long solo to fill the empty space, and the moment burned itself into my brain like a snapshot: Deena sitting up in her bed like a hospital-gowned Madonna, Peg solid and glowing with the baby in her arms, looking happier than I'd seen her in months, Rose closing herself off from all of us, and behind her, although I don't know why this stays with me, the room's rumpled second bed. Whoever it belonged to, I imagined her creeping the halls, too sore to walk well but preferring pain to the tensions of a family that wasn't hers. Jude's fallen out of the picture as cleanly as if she'd never been there, because it was all about Deena right then, and the baby, and of course Peg.

"You better give that baby back before you try to steal her," Deena said.

"Too late. Sorry."

"Here," Jude said. "I haven't had a turn."

"You have to support the head," Deena said.

"I know that."

"Well, excuse me for worrying. She's the only one I've got."

Jude sat back down, making a show out of supporting the baby's head.

Peg came back and leaned beside me on the windowsill. She caught me watching her and smiled – not the kind of smile you decide on but the kind that comes on its own. With no warning, we were in love again. We were perfect. The family was quiet for a while and I let myself believe that since Peg and I were happy they must be too. Then Deena started talking again, unable to hear silence without pouring herself into it. She spun tales about the apartment she was going to rent, the job she'd find the second the baby turned three months, the woman she knew who did day care and had promised she'd have a slot open by then.

"Everything's going to be simple for you, isn't it?" Rose said. "You wait. Babies are hard."

"Hey, thanks for the good wishes, Mom."

"They are. They're hard and then they get older and they get harder. This is the easy stage. She's hungry, you feed her. She's dirty, you change her. If nothing else works, you get off your ass and you walk her. It's afterward it gets complicated. You're going to have to learn to think things through for a change."

Deena met Rose's eyes as if they were holding a staring contest, but even she couldn't think of anything to say.

"You think this is a walk in the park, don't you? Hey, so what if your old mom had a hard time. You're too smart for that, aren't you? It's going to be nothing for you. But this kid—"

She nodded at the baby, sleeping red-faced and perfect in Jude's arms.

"This kid what?" Deena said.

"This kid nothing. You'll find out soon enough."

There was a space of several breaths where no one said anything. I leaned closer to Peg. I'd have hidden behind her if I'd thought I could get away with it. Then something shifted in her – her breath, the line of her back and neck, as if she was rearranging her ordinary connections, becoming a therapist. Her voice, when she started to talk, was softer and more deliberate than the voice I was used to.

"You're worried about her, aren't you?" she asked Rose.

I caught a glimpse of the way Peg remade herself, over and over again, as somebody other than Rose, picking her way past the sharp rocks and the quick anger.

"Of course I'm worried about her," Rose said. "I'd be a driveling idiot not to be worried about her."

I wasn't sure which *her* they meant, the baby or Deena, but it amounted to the same thing right then.

Rose turned to Deena, shying away from whatever direction Peg had been trying to move in.

"You don't do right by this kid, I'll call Child Protection myself."

"Jesus, Mom. I love you too."

"You see if I don't."

"What, you think I'm going to take her out of here and whack her head on the sidewalk? That's my kid there." She nodded toward the baby in Jude's arms. "That's my baby."

I waited for Rose to say that at some point every mother wants to whack her kid's head against some solid object, but she just stared out the window as if she'd never been any part of the conversation. Maybe every mother doesn't feel that way. How would I know? Peg stared out the door and became the everyday Peg I was used to, but I didn't pull away from her, and I didn't think she pulled away from me. How do we explain the decisions that make themselves inside our minds and our bodies? Something had changed, either between us or in the two of us separately. Jude hummed something unrecognizable and rocked the baby. The rest of us stared at different parts of the room, either looking for something to say or not even bothering to look. Not even Deena broke the silence.

Eventually Peg said we had to get going. Rose pushed herself out of her chair and said they should go too. Jude handed the baby back to Deena, and they were awkward about it, as if they had gravel rolled inside the blanket and were trying to keep it from spilling.

We threaded our way through the halls, following blue arrows to the elevator. Peg's hand touched my back for a second and then it was gone. I might have caught her eye but Rose was talking.

"And what kind of name is that anyway?" she said as if she were picking up on something one of us had just said. "It makes her sound like a stripper, for god's sake."

Jude put a hand over her mouth and giggled as if she expected to be scolded for it – wishing, I think, that she came from the kind of family where she would have been. Peg whacked herself on the head in a you-idiot gesture.

"I didn't ask. What the hell did she name her?"

I punched the elevator button.

"Krystal."

Rose punched the button, hard, as if I hadn't just done it.

"With a K."

The elevator didn't come any faster for Rose than it did for me.

"*And* a Y."

"It always has a Y," Jude said.

Rose ignored her.

"You're the expert," she said to Peg. "You tell me. What did I do wrong with that kid? How was I supposed to get some sense into her head?"

"Hey, don't drag me into this."

"It's a professional secret or something? I'm not supposed to ask?"

"She's my sister, for chrissake."

"Believe me, I know she's your sister."

"So you're my mother."

"I got that one right too."

"So I can't go around diagnosing my family."

"Then what good is it, what you do?"

I could see Peg struggling toward some sort of answer – something softer than Rose's question – then she shook her head and said, "It's a living, okay?"

Rose would have said something more but the elevator doors opened on a crowded car and we layered ourselves in at the front, facing forward, closing ourselves into our separate thought bubbles. Our separate no-thought bubbles. Then the doors opened and we piled into the lobby and Rose managed to stop us right where the crowd had to split and flow around us.

"So what am I supposed to do now?" she said.

It came out like an accusation and Peg shook her head.

"What you'd do anyway. Help out where you can. Show her whatever she'll let you. Try not to let her push your buttons."

"Fat chance of that happening. That's your professional opinion?"

"I can't have a professional opinion. She's my sister. That's what I think, is all it is."

I waited for Rose to make a six-years-of-college-and-you-don't-have-a-professional-opinion speech, but she didn't. She never said she was proud of Peg's education, but she never made fun of it either, and when anyone in that family cut the others some slack you had to take notice. So I took notice. I let the tide of Rose's complaining pride buoy me up and we floated outside, the four of us, into that clean air we'd borrowed from Canada, the air I hadn't allowed myself to enjoy when we were in the parking ramp, and it let me believe in hope, in renewal, in second chances. I believed that Deena would split the skin of her old self and step forth steady and reliable, transformed into the mother we all wanted her to be. She'd find the job she wanted, the apartment, the day-care slot. Peg and I were back in tune, so what could the world do but jump in and sing backup?

Rose and Jude left us, turning east toward Rose's car, and Peg took my arm. I felt self-conscious about it, as if I'd turned into the balding half of a sixty-five-year-old straight couple, but all the same it felt right. It felt wonderful. Deena had shoved us one rung up the generational ladder. Neither of us had a clue what that meant yet, but I pressed Peg's hand between my arm and my ribs and it was enough.

I remember those months after Krys was born as a kind of holiday, all golden light and green leaves – no rain, no mosquito bites, no cold weather tightening its grip on the city. As mysteriously as we'd started fighting, we'd stopped, although we were cautious still, afraid one of us would say the wrong thing.

The first time Deena left Krys with us, I wouldn't hold her. Her neck was made of spun glass. What if for half a second I forgot to support her head?

Peg walked her up and down as if nothing could hurt her, cooing while Krys squalled, telling her to sleep, to sleep, to sleep, until finally, as if the words were what made a difference, she did sleep, and Peg held her out to me.

"Here. Rest her on your arm."

"Don't. I'll drop her."

"She'll be fine. Come on. Hurry or she'll wake up."

I let Peg put her in my arms and sat frozen on the couch.

"She doesn't weigh anything," I whispered.

"Walk her a while. You'd be surprised what she weighs."

I didn't dare. I sat like a boulder, looking into her squinched-up little face and feeling something I didn't know to call love but that swept through me all the same, rearranging my molecules too quietly for me to resist.

"You look nice like that," Peg said.

"Don't laugh. I'm no good at this."

"I'm not laughing."

She sat next to me and our arms pressed against each other while the two of us stared into Krys's unconscious face. It was an odd way of being together, joined and separated by this sleeping infant, but the old spark jumped between us. She mouthed a kiss at me and nodded upstairs, toward the bedroom. It had been months since we'd tried that and my entire body said yes.

I gave Krys back to her – I was terrified of carrying her – and we tiptoed upstairs, lowered her into the crib, and snuck across the hall, closing the door behind us as if Krys would have understood what we were up to even if she'd been awake to hear.

For the first time in what seemed like ages, I took flight with Peg – it hadn't crossed my mind that I might not – and afterward she pulled the covers over us, sank into her pillow, and touched my cheek. Nothing major, just a small, unnecessary gesture that mattered as much to me as the sex itself.

It was weeks before I was brave enough to hold Krys and walk at the same time, but even when she still terrified me I was flattered to have her at our house, flattered to be included in this thing that sisters did for each other in real families. I was more than flattered. As a kid, I'd studied the yellow glow that spilled out of other people's windows and I'd known, with a kid's certainty, that the families behind those windows were happier than we were at my parents' house. I never once stopped to think that the light in our house spilled out of the same power lines as theirs and must have looked just as yellow from the street.

With Krys in our lives, I felt like I'd moved inside that yellow glow; like Peg and I both had. It wasn't just the two of us anymore. There was something timeless about taking care of this infant, as if we were reaching back to the first humans huddled around their fires and into the future through the memory of a child who was still too young to shape memories. I wondered if my own family hadn't stumbled into a pocket of time like this when I was still too young to remember it. I don't know if it's sadder to believe that they did and then lost it or that they never, even for a few weeks, knew what that was like before they dragged themselves into a Saturday morning, hungover and surrounded by dirty diapers and spit-up rags, with me screaming in my crib.

I don't want to romanticize Krys any more than I want to romanticize what Peg and I had. She wasn't an easy baby. Even after we'd fed her and burped her and changed her, she cried. She cried while we walked her and she cried while we rocked her. And whenever she wasn't crying, we were waiting for her to start. But even so, she brought us moments of pure bliss. She'd fall asleep with her head just below my shoulder and one hand clutching my shirt, and I could feel consciousness drain out of her until she lay against me as softly as a strand of grass. Her head radiated heat, and I'd touch that hot, downy head with one finger and think, *I was capable of this once*, without stopping to ask myself what *this* was. Trust, I suppose. A kind of love I could barely imagine even as I watched it. This complete abandonment of herself to someone else. Nothing in my life – not the memory of my own childhood, not the babysitting I'd done in my teens, not even those moments with Peg when I kicked loose from myself – had prepared me for the way Krys reached inside me. I'd heard new mothers say, "There's no feeling like it in the world," but it had only been words until then. Noise.

There *was* no feeling like it in the world. A hand that doesn't stretch the width of your palm grabs a chunk of your shirt, or your lip, or your ear, and you know she could just as easily be grabbing the neighbors' dog or a wad of newspaper but even so you're ready to turn your whole life inside out for her. It's how we're wired. It's why the human race survives. But even if it is just wiring, it still struck me as deeply personal. There I was, loving someone I couldn't expect to get anything back from. I wasn't her mother or grandmother. I wasn't even her aunt, really. She owed me nothing.

I learned from Krys to touch Peg for no better reason than that I wanted to. I learned to press Peg's hand closer to my face when she laid it there. Because we both seemed to overflow sometimes, and the only thing we could do with it was touch.

Baby equipment sprouted in odd corners of our house like mushrooms: bottles, packs of diapers, doll-sized socks, and I picked them up without thinking they meant anything. Not even Peg's coffee cups and abandoned clothes bothered me. Or they did bother me, but I didn't attach any more meaning to them than that she was the kind of person who left things in strange places. I either picked them up or I didn't pick them up, and for the most part I stopped keeping track.

Even the money mattered less. If Peg bought a pair of slacks she didn't need, what the hell, it wasn't a car. It wasn't even an expensive pair of slacks. Money wasn't that tight, and I learned to remind myself of this.

Krys got older and cried less. She smiled, then she laughed. She crowed and kicked her feet if we made quacking sounds. The house sprouted toys, sippy cups, all the bright pieces of plastic that babies seem to create simply by breathing. Once, after we'd dropped Krys off at Deena's, Peg stopped in the middle of fastening her seat belt, the buckle suspended over her hip as if the words were important enough to keep her hands from working.

"We're very lucky," she said. "You know that?"

I did know. She seemed to be touching me without an inch of skin making contact, and I was happy enough that I had no idea what to do with it.

I still thought Peg was too far away sometimes, but I'd started telling myself that no one could stretch those perfect moments out forever, and it's odd how comforting that *no one* was, as if happiness was some kind of competition, as if someone down the street being happier would turn the life we'd carved out for ourselves into not enough anymore. As if the rest of the world having less would make us into millionaires. I still suspected our share wasn't big enough, and I was blown away that we had any at all.

Deena wasn't one of the people I measured our happiness against, but if I'd given it any thought I might have voted for her to pursue a little less happiness and a little more stability. She was always bounding off after something new, something male, something unflawed by the problems you notice once you've had a close look. Still, she seemed steady enough after Krys was born. She hauled herself out of bed every morning, dropped Krys off at day care and punched the clock at work, and she came back to pick her up every afternoon. Not the day care she'd planned on, not the apartment or the job she'd talked about, but plans were like that with Deena. She made them and she believed in them and she forgot about them and made new plans. But she kept Krys fed and dressed and unbruised, and if she wasn't what we'd have constructed if someone had given us the parts – well, which of us was? Peg took to telling me how well Deena was doing, how Krys had settled her down, and I let myself drift in the current of her belief, even if it did seem to me that Deena drank more than was strictly necessary. Peg was the expert. I overreacted when people drank. I knew that. And people did sometimes drink without bringing the roof down on their heads. At least Deena enjoyed it. She made it look good. My parents drank with all the joy of two people hammering nails – whack, that one's done; whack, that's another down. As if drinking was one more miserable goddamn job they'd been saddled with.

I told myself there was no point in planning for a disaster that might never happen. Deena loved Krys. She read to her. She worried over her. She managed. What more, realistically, could I ask? Even when she got pregnant again and the father disappeared from her life—

Okay, for a while there it got rocky. She wept. She ranted. She called to tell us where his car was parked at 2 a.m. and who lived just down the street, and she'd known he was looking at her. She'd known it. He'd said he wasn't, but she'd known it.

And then the storm blew through. Before the morning sickness had even stopped, she swore she couldn't remember why he'd seemed to matter.

It wasn't long afterward that Rose died – just blinked out at work one day while she was kneeling down to pull jammed paper out of the copy machine – and even then Deena stayed steady.

She and Jude both pitched in like adults. Peg filled out the forms, made the calls, paid the bills, but Jude cleaned the house so it could go on the market and Deena sorted, sold, threw out and turned up unexpectedly with an armload of whatever she decided someone would want. One Saturday, she showed up at our door and I heard her tell Peg that Krys was in the car, she couldn't come in.

"Remember this, though?" she asked. "You are now the keeper of the hammer Mom threw when she chased the Peeping Tom."

"I'll treasure it," Peg said.

"Be sure you do."

Peg came in with a cupcake tin and a box of Christmas ornaments as well as the hammer, and she held the hammer up to show me.

"I'd almost forgotten that thing with the hammer."

"Did she hit him?"

"Yeah, well, you know what family stories are like. She never threw it. But she did chase him. And she was waving it." She set the other stuff down so she could appreciate the hammer properly.

"I'll tell you this: he never came back."

"We should get it mounted and hang it on the wall."

She abandoned it on the dining-room table and I left it there for a few days, in a place of honor, before I put it in the toolbox.

I don't know what Jude got to remember Rose by, but they didn't fight over it, I know that much.

She took the cats in. It struck me as an adult thing for her to do.

Jude was newly married by then, but still young enough that she was playing house more than keeping one. Every time we saw her she talked sheets, towels, furniture, a throw rug she'd bought, as if each addition was going to make her life whole. Peg liked to pick stuff up for her – nonstick cookie sheets; a butter dish; a long-handled pink duster which for reasons I never understood they both thought was spectacular. They could have been furnishing a dollhouse.

The other thing Jude talked about was recipes: what Dex would eat, what Dex wouldn't eat, as if she was afraid that we'd forget she had this man, this husband, in her life, and that she was Happy, with a capital H. Dex was a decent enough guy – reliable, skinny, uninspiring. I couldn't imagine anyone falling in love with him, but I always figured Jude fell in love with the married state at least as much as with the man himself.

They had an apartment above a laundromat and the plan was to save until they had the down payment on a house. Rose's house should've given them that when it sold, but Rose had taken out a second mortgage and the neighborhood had gone downhill. In the end, the money didn't amount to much.

Then Jude got pregnant and forget the sheets, forget the recipes, forget the house even – there'd be houses later. She'd been looking in other people's windows too, I think, and the whole time she was pregnant she glowed as if she'd swallowed the source of that yellow light. Peg stopped buying her household stuff and bought knit booties, baby blankets, bottles.

Krys was four and Jude and Deena's babies were on either side of a year when the whole structure fell apart. Deena asked Jude and Dex to keep the kids for a weekend, and when she didn't show up on Sunday Jude called to ask if we'd heard from her. I yelled downstairs for Peg to pick up the phone.

"All she told me was she'd met someone," Jude said. "And you know Deena, you'd think she'd never met a man before.

That must've been Thursday, because Dex was working overtime. So I thought maybe she told you something."

"Not a word."

"I should've asked something, I know I should've asked something, but she was always meeting someone, and it was always, you know, this is the one. I don't know, I guess I pretty much stopped listening. I mean, this guy could've told her he was Jack the Ripper and I wouldn't know it."

We played twenty questions: have you called her apartment? Have you gone over there? Have you tried the hospitals, the police, the highway patrol?

When we got to Jude and Dex's, Krys was sitting on the living-room floor and shrieking – she wanted *her* bed, she wanted her mommy – and the three of us watched her with the same urge that makes people turn their heads as they drive past car wrecks. She launched a book at us and it bounced off Peg's leg and flapped to the floor. We all pretended not to notice, except for the cats, who streaked into the other room. I'd never seen Jude or Peg do that with the kids before.

Krys considered us for a second, measuring the quality of our attention, then she whacked a toy radio against the rug and waited to see what we'd do.

So did I. We did nothing.

The radio played "Three Blind Mice" in soulless electronic notes. She whacked it some more and started howling again. She wanted her mommy. I wanted her too, and damn near as desperately.

The moment seemed to stretch on forever, then Peg squatted down in front of Krys and asked something quietly – I couldn't hear what. Krys stopped shrieking and shook her head. "Three Blind Mice" played. She held the radio suspended, ready to start whacking it again. The song ended.

"I understand that you're angry," Peg said, "but I don't think your mom'll get here tonight."

Krys raised the radio to throw it, I think, or to give it another good whack, and Peg reached to stop her and got hit on the arm. "Three Blind Mice" started up again and Krys kicked and wailed for Deena. Peg got her arms around her somehow, pinning her while she flailed and yelled "I hate you."

"Three Blind Mice" played.

Jude and I gawked.

As I remember it, it took forever for Krys to stop fighting and simply cry, but when she did Peg shifted her hold and rocked her. A long, long time later, she picked Krys up and carried her to bed, and they were beautiful together, Krys wilted against Peg's shoulder and Peg bending her head to whisper shushing sounds. Jude and I watched in silence, then the two of us cleared up the living room and waited for Peg to come back. It was a long room, running the full width of the laundromat downstairs, and Krys had thrown toys in all directions. I flattened the crumpled pages of the book Krys had flung at us – a dog jumping, a boy in shorts holding a stick for it, one of those upbeat things that people got rid of at garage sales, full of kids in relentlessly clean summer clothes with mothers who never disappear.

"Where's Dex?" I asked.

"He drove over there to see if the caretaker'd let him inside."

There, of course, being Deena's.

"He should've been back by now."

She was turning the toy radio in her hands and hit the button again. "Three Blind Mice".

"God, I hate that song."

"Give it here."

She handed it over and I shoved it under a couch cushion. It chimed away at us from under the stuffing.

"Want me to sit on it?" I said. "I think I could do it in."

Jude giggled – that old gesture, hiding her mouth behind her hand as if it was no fun to laugh without someone to hide it from. Then she dropped the hand and let the giggle drop away with it.

"I am so scared for her."

"It's too soon for that."

She nodded, grateful for any reason to put that off.

"Dex would've called—"

She left the reasons he would have called unsaid, and I said, Sure, he would have, although I doubted it. If he'd found anything – and I didn't let my imagination run past the blankness of *anything* – he'd have the police to talk to, the caretaker to deal with. And Dex might be the kind of guy who'd call to say "I'm running late", but he wouldn't call to say "This is awful. I just had to talk to you." Peg might, or I might, but not Dex, and I let myself feel sorry for Jude because she didn't know to miss that imaginary call.

The radio shut itself off and I dug it out of the couch. We were out of things to pick up and sat facing the blank TV screen. "Three Blind Mice" played in my head. I'd never noticed before what a horrible song it was.

"If there's anything you need us to do till she does show up—"

Jude shook her head.

"I know their day care—"

I wondered whether Deena paid her day care at the beginning of the week or the end. Or did people pay that by the month, like rent? Should I offer to help out now or wait and let Peg bring it up?

"What time was she supposed to pick them up?"

"Noon, one, somewhere in there."

It was dark out – late enough that I was thinking about calling in sick the next day. I almost never did, but my shift started early and getting enough sleep was always an issue. I liked to think I could steal a day for myself if I needed one.

"I always worried about her," Jude said, "but I never thought – not something like this."

We weren't sure what "something like this" was yet, but I nodded. I wouldn't have thought it either.

Eventually Peg joined us.

"God, can that kid fight sleep. I thought she was out three separate times."

"She's a hard one to get to sleep anyway," Jude said. As if only she knew about kids. As if Krys had never slept at our house. As if staking out an area where she was the expert would turn her into the older sister.

"So was Deena."

It was an eerily normal conversation.

"A mind of her own, that one," Jude said.

"Ya, well, she's going to need it."

Jude made a noise that sounded like disapproval. I waited for Peg to argue but she just leaned against the arm of the couch. The conversation narrowed down to a few words, a silence, a hum, a few more words, all of us just filling time.

Eventually Dex came upstairs with one bag of clothes and another one of toys.

"I didn't know their favorites," he said. "I just, you know, grabbed some stuff."

He held the bags away from his body, looking baffled by this foreign language of girls' clothes, girls' toys. Jude got up to take them from him with the automatic meshing of two people who know each other's moves. This was love the way two football players feel love, one passing the ball and the other one receiving it. Love the way cars on the freeway make space for each other to keep from crashing. Watching them, I believed they'd stay together. I believed that was enough. Not enough for me and Peg necessarily, but I didn't mind if it worked for them.

Peg said we should go and we did get up, but instead of leaving we all bunched up by the door and argued about whether to call the police. It wasn't the kind of argument where anyone got mad, or even took a side and stayed on it. We jumped around randomly, all of us arguing against whatever we'd been in favor of a minute before. In the end we didn't call, not so much because we decided not to as because we couldn't decide that we should. It was easier to wait. It was less frightening.

"What do we tell Krys if Deena isn't home tomorrow?" Jude asked – the youngest again, now that we were leaving. Peg and I had gotten as far as the hall just outside the door and the question came out at a whisper: to keep the possibility from Krys if she was awake. To keep it from herself.

"Just don't lie to her," Peg said. "You can say you hope she'll come back, you can say you don't know, but don't lie to her."

"She'll want more than that."

"We all want more than that. Don't lie to her."

We walked downstairs. I took Peg's hand and squeezed and she squeezed back to let me know she was there. It wasn't what I wanted, exactly, but it was what was available.

"She'll be all right," I said. "It's just Deena having a Deena moment."

Months went by, though, with no Deena. Her credit card bills showed a string of charges moving south and then west, and we took that as a sign that she was alive. Jude and Dex absorbed the kids into their lives, and they complained about Deena every chance they got, but I never once heard them complain about the kids. Peg and I took on the role of the newly single father, writing checks, taking the kids every other weekend, but it was Jude and Dex we brought them back to on Sunday afternoon, Jude and Dex who made the money stretch.

When Deena's rent came due, we emptied her apartment, opening every piece of folded paper we found, looking for something that might tell us why she'd gone, who she'd gone with, whether she was safe. It felt like snooping to read it all and like willful stupidity not to. When we didn't find any hints we shoved everything in boxes and pretended it made sense to keep it. We packed the girls' stuff into Jake's old room and wrestled Jake's crib into Jude and Dex's. We hauled Deena's bed to our garage and left it until Peg noticed a border of mouse droppings along the base and we dragged it out to the alley, leaning it on the fence beside the garbage bin for the city to cart off. The boxes of odds and ends landed on our porch – old bits of makeup, forks and knives, cigarette lighters, a brown leather shoulder bag with a mirror and a penknife in the bottom, the torn-off "Keep This Portion for Your Records" section of old electric bills. All the broken bits of a life.

What I remember most about that time isn't the way Deena's absence weighed on us, although it did. What I remember is exhaustion illuminated by tiny explosions of bliss that were like fireworks shot off in a fog. Krys would hurl herself at one of us for a hug. The babies would fall asleep in our arms. For seconds at a time, we were whole and our lives were perfect.

By the time Deena did show up, six months had gone by. She knocked on Jude and Dex's door, checked what she could see of the apartment from the doorway and asked where the hell her kids were.

"That's it?" Jude said when she'd pulled herself together enough to say anything at all. "You just waltz in here and say 'Where the hell are my kids?' We thought you were dead."

Which wasn't true, strictly speaking, but we hadn't been able to keep from wondering.

"Next best thing," she said. "I was in California. I tried to call – I really did try to call – but it got complicated. Everything got complicated. You going to ask me in?"

Jude stood aside to let her in and Dex wandered over from the kitchen sink, where he'd taken the drainpipe apart. He had his sweatshirt sleeves pushed up and something greasy smeared across the back of one hand.

"I'm going to have to buy a new J-bend," he said. "That one's shot."

"As if she'd dropped the kids off yesterday," Jude said when she told us about it later. "And I'm thinking, 'Did I make this whole thing up?'"

Jude trailed after Deena into her own living room and they sat there as stiffly as a couple outside a divorce court, waiting for the bailiff to call their names. Dex leaned in the archway to the living room, the wrench still dangling from one hand.

"So where are the kids?" Deena said again, but instead of answering her Jude talked lawyers and judges, custody and abandonment, the termination of legal rights, while Deena cried.

"They're my kids," Deena said.

"Whose kids were they in October? Whose kids were they at Christmas?"

Deena stopped crying.

"You have no idea what it was like."

"You're damn right we don't," Dex said.

Deena didn't so much as flick an eye toward him. She left the tears on her cheek like the headline on a supermarket tabloid: "Mother Cries for Missing Kids". She told them how she'd ended up on the West Coast, stranded and broke, and she'd meant to send for the kids the whole time but nothing had worked out like it was supposed to. She was thinking about their best interest. She was protecting them.

"Even the dry cleaner," Jude said, "after thirty days, you don't pick your clothes up, they're gone. You lose them."

"My kids aren't the damn dry cleaning. You don't think I cried for those kids every day?"

"Fat lot of good that did them."

"They need me."

"They needed you in December. You want to know what Christmas was like around here?"

Deena's eyes got teary again. They overflowed and she smeared makeup across her cheeks.

"Look, I screwed up, okay? You don't think I know that? But I'm back. I'm going to make it up to them. You want to pound me on the head with everything I did wrong, fine,

I probably deserve that, but those kids need me. And I need them."

"Until you need something else more," Jude said.

Deena cried harder.

"Where are they?"

"They're at high school graduation. Where the hell do you think they are?"

"They're at Peg's, aren't they?"

"I'm not telling you where they are."

Which was as good as saying yes.

They got louder from there. Deena shouted that Jude had always been jealous of her. Jude listed everything in Deena's life that she'd never been jealous of.

They were still hashing that out when Peg and I clomped upstairs, bringing the kids home. Dex opened the door for us, the wrench still dangling from one hand, giving us a clear view of Deena and Jude, frozen in the living room, their heads turned toward us.

"This might not be the best time," Dex said, nodding down at Krys as if she couldn't see him every bit as well as we could. As if she couldn't see her mother. He was talking to me more than to Peg – he'd decided long ago that I was an honorary brother-in-law and I never had figured out how I felt about it. All I could think to do right then was look through the open door, then look down at Krys as if I could see through her head and measure how much she understood and what she'd think if we turned around and hustled her back to the car.

"I don't think we have a choice about this," Peg said.

Dex might have argued but Krys marched past him, drawn to drama as surely as her mother always had been. No one else moved. I thought, oddly, of Rose, of the blood vessel that split open in her head, letting all the silence pulse out of her. Then Deena said, "Hello, baby."

Her voice was strikingly quiet – controlled, almost casual.

Peg moved toward the living room in Krys's wake, and Dex and I followed. Jake was in Dex's arms and the wrench was gone, although I hadn't seen either of these things happen. I had Kerri on my hip. She was at that age where she clung like a tick – that age where she couldn't have known anymore that Deena was her mother. It had been too long. We lined up in the archway like the audience at a play, waiting to see what Krys would do.

Deena knelt down and opened her arms.

"You going to come to Mommy?"

Krys did, but not like a kid who'd spent weeks crying herself to sleep for lack of this woman. She moved crabwise, offering Deena the bony angles, the least welcoming parts of the human body, and when Deena wrapped her arms around her she stood inside them with all the warmth and give of a fire hydrant.

Deena put one hand on each of Krys's cheeks. It was a beautiful gesture – gentle, protective, the gesture made by the mother that every mother wants to be.

"Baby, I missed you so much."

Krys stood frozen. Tears ran down Deena's face.

"Know what we're going to do now?" Deena said. "Mommy's going to find an apartment just like the one we used to have and we're going to live together, you and me and Kerri."

Krys looked at her, not giving out a thing.

"You remember our old place? Remember that bear lamp you had? You used to kiss it goodnight?"

"It's not a bear."

"We'll find one just like it. Would you like that?"

"It's not a *bear*."

Deena's hands were on Krys's shoulders now. The gesture was less perfect. The kid wasn't giving her the right lines.

"You want to come live with Mommy?"

"Jude's my mommy now."

Deena let her hands drop away and turned to Jude.

"You taught her that."

"What do you expect, Deena? You disappear out of their lives, you think I can just stick them in the freezer, do the suspended animation thing?"

"They're my *kids*."

"Then you better get yourself a damn good lawyer, cause I'll fight you for them."

It was quiet for a second. I looked at Jude and saw what had probably been there for months without me noticing it: she'd come into herself, as if all her life she'd been waiting for the world to ask something difficult of her and finally it had.

"You could be my mommy too," Krys said.

Deena ran a hand absently over Krys's head.

"Yeah, baby."

"And Kerri's."

Deena patted her cheek. The gesture was more real, I think, than the perfect one. It promised less, but it didn't move me the way the perfect one had. She got up off the floor like a much older woman – the way I do today – and crossed to where I stood with Kerri still in my arms. My mind rushed ahead of what was happening and I believed that if I handed Kerri over Deena would run out the door with her. I believed that we'd all chase down the stairs after her and that we'd lose Kerri if we didn't catch up, but we'd all pull at Kerri and hurt her if we did. In spite of which I couldn't imagine saying no to Deena. Who was I to tell her she couldn't take her own baby? I was still wondering what I'd do when instead of holding out her arms she reached to touch Kerri's face the way she had Krys's.

Kerri burrowed into my shoulder and hid.

Deena stood there for what seemed like a long time, looking at the back of Kerri's head, reading the future in the wisps of her hair. Then she turned to Jude.

"You'll take good care of them for me?"

Jude nodded.

"Promise."

Jude promised, and they measured each other until Deena finally nodded back as if she'd extracted something Jude hadn't wanted to give.

She planted herself in front of Dex.

"You ever lay a hand on my kids, I'll kill you."

He stared at her as if she'd suggested dismembering and eating them.

"I swear I will. You don't believe me, just try it."

She held the moment like an actor, and we waited.

"Deena?" Peg said. It was the first time in an age that I'd noticed the small, trapped sound of her voice.

Deena turned.

"We've got your stuff still."

She made it almost a question.

"Burn it, okay? Just fuckin' burn it."

And she left, not slamming the door or yelling her way down the stairs, just leaving it open so we'd hear her footsteps all the way down. Someone said "Jesus", but quietly. I set Kerri down.

"Are we going to live with my mommy-mommy?" Krys said.

"No, hon."

Krys accepted that as if she'd been asking about popsicles – are they orange or are they grape? – giving out no hint of what she felt. Maybe she didn't know herself. She went to the window to watch for Deena on the sidewalk below. I would've liked to join her but I couldn't get that far. I seemed to be standing knee-deep in wet cement. It wasn't that I couldn't move or even that I shouldn't, but it did seem like an awful lot of work and where would I end up but someplace not that different from where I already was?

Krys turned away from the window, leaving a bubbled splotch where she'd laid her lips against the glass.

"And it's not a bear," she said to nobody in particular. "'Tsa panda."

"That actually is a kind of bear," Peg said. I don't know why. To leave Krys with the sense that Deena really had been paying attention, maybe, or only because it seemed like something Krys should know.

"'Tsa *panda,*" Krys yelled.

"'Okay, sweets. It's a panda."

"It is. 'Tsa panda."

"You want a hug, babe?"

Krys wrapped her arms around herself so she was all elbows and thorns and knobby shoulders.

"Okay," Peg said. "Bad idea. No hug."

I bought takeout at a Vietnamese place on Lake Street that night, and we sat up with Jude and Dex long after the kids were in bed while Jude told us everything Deena had said, and everything she'd said, and everything Deena had said back, then hashing out all the moves Deena might make and the countermoves we could make if she did. It was like playing chess when you couldn't predict the ways the pieces would move. Was Deena prone to legal actions or kidnapping, emotional scenes in front of the kids or suicide? Did she move two squares forward and one to the side or throw the whole board on the floor and stomp on the pieces?

"I don't think she's got the patience for lawyers," Peg said.

"Or the money," Dex said.

"Or the money."

That left us with the more disturbing possibilities. We picked at the last bits of food and when the food was gone we gathered up the cardboard cartons and extra napkins and soy sauce packets and threw them all away. Jude started crying. She was still holding the garbage bag we'd thrown everything into.

"I shouldn't feel this way," she said, "but it's not just the kids. I hate having her back is what it is. I just hate having her back."

Dex came up behind her and put his hands on her shoulders. No more than that: just stood there, a little embarrassed, a little awkward, but touching her in spite of that. If I'd been Jude, I'd have grabbed that moment and wept out every ounce of sadness that had ever crossed my life, because if she hadn't chosen a partner with a gift for closeness she'd at least found one who was willing to wade through his own discomfort and touch her shoulders when she needed him.

All she did, though, was smear her tears with one hand and listen to Peg saying Deena'd always been hard on her, it was natural for her to feel that way. I'd have wept over that too: absolution, and from a relative. Dex lifted his hands off her shoulders, took the garbage bag from her and tied the top. She stopped crying. The moment was over, but that's all any of us have. Moments. Seconds, hours – weeks if we're lucky. Flashes of time when we're more than ourselves and can let another person touch us. Flashes of time when we give ourselves over to someone else the way Jake and Kerri still could, the way Krys was learning not to do. And it lasts until the other person reaches for the garbage bag. If you wait long enough, and if you're wise enough or lucky enough, or maybe both, it happens again.

Peg was still talking about how hard Deena'd been on Jude, and Jude was saying, "I thought it was just me," and, "I thought everyone would say it was my fault." Dex took the garbage out, and I came up behind Peg so I could wrap my arms around her shoulders and rest my chin on the top of her head. It wasn't one of those moments. I wasn't overwhelmed by love and I didn't become more than myself. But I did, in that moment, love her, and I was happy enough with the two of us to think that whatever we had was enough. I could have stopped there, in that moment, and said yes, it was worth the price. What we had was worth the price.

Nothing does stop, though. I unwrapped my arms from Peg's shoulders. Dex came back from taking out the garbage. Peg and I went home, and for weeks we were edgy with each other, as if we each knew a word that would sling us back to that awful time after we bought the house.

For those same weeks, Deena showed up to see the kids, sometimes bringing presents, sometimes weeping and telling them how much she'd missed them. She told Krys she'd buy her a pony when she and Kerri came to live with her. After Deena left, Jude tried to explain that Deena had only been talking about something she'd like to do, not something she really could do, but Krys wouldn't believe her. What kid would? She'd go live with Deena and have a pony. A spotted one. When Kerri got bigger she could have one too.

"I don't know if I said the right thing," Jude told us a couple of days later.

We showed up at Jude and Dex's almost as often as Deena, as if the weight of numbers would pull the kids to our side. Because the family had divided up into opposing teams: us against Deena, Deena against us, all of us competing for the girls, with Jake off on the sidelines somewhere and too young to know it yet. We sat on the floor and played with them and tried to make life look normal – or better than normal – and after they were in bed we settled in at the kitchen table to let Jude count out Deena's latest offenses. Somehow we always sat in the kitchen, as if getting too comfortable would tempt us to let down our guard.

"The thing of it is, is she made me mad," Jude said when she told us about the pony. "I mean, there I am, I'm looking at Krys, and none of this is her fault, I know that, but I swear I could hear Deena's voice coming out of her mouth just as sure as if she'd planted a tape recorder in there. I said, 'Listen, Deena says a lot of things, and she means them when she says them, but most of them never happen, okay? They're just talk, so you have to get used to that. You can't count on her.'"

She looked away, looked back.

"Sometimes I wish she had died."

Her voice belonged to the teenage younger sister she still was, even if it was only for a few more months.

"I don't really mean that. She just makes me so mad sometimes."

Peg made a small, sympathetic sound – it's okay, it's just a thought, you're doing fine. I nodded – a bit more of yes, you're doing fine, like Peg's backup band. Dex went into a tirade about how Deena never thought about anybody but herself, and even if what he said was true he still sounded achingly young and self-righteous. The world was such a simple place. Deena was wrong, and that meant we had no reason to doubt ourselves. I listened to him with at most half my brain. It was late, and the lateness had wrapped around us like a fog, softening his outline and Jude's so that instead of pushing me away his narrowness seemed like just a part of him – eyes, hair, mouth, tendency to self-righteousness. It wasn't like Peg and I had a handle on perfection. It came to me all neatly packaged in words that Jude and Dex were heroes, taking the kids in the way they had, and I was more deeply moved by that thought than by the actual people sitting with me at the table. A set of words had formed in my brain and projected Jude and Dex onto a movie screen, where they swept me along in a tide of feeling that was unobstructed by their ordinariness and annoying habits. I loved Jude and Dex at that moment as completely and as ineffectively as anyone has ever loved a sunset or a piece of music or any of a thousand other things that we can't touch and can't eat and can't even keep from slipping away but that fill us just the same. I was filled by them and speechless with love.

"And what about when she's been drinking," Jude said, Rose-like, as if it followed from something one of us had just said. "If I let her in she upsets the kids and if I don't let her in she'll stand out there and yell, and that'll upset the kids too. And if I call the cops, which I probably should, the kids'll hear all of that. So any way we go, we lose. The kids lose."

Peg and I murmured, as if we'd rehearsed it, that we weren't sure, that we didn't know. We shrank away from endorsing any decisive act as if it was the wicked stepmother's poison apple offered to us a second time and thank you, no, but we'd learned that trick.

"You don't let her in," Dex said.

He was so young that it hurt to look at him, sitting at his kitchen table and trying on the role of patriarch, clunking around in it like a boy who'd stuck his palm-sized feet into Daddy's shoes. At any normal time I have no patience for men playing I'm-the-head-of-the-household, but I was oddly touched by it that night. This was how Dex had seen things done all his life. This was what he thought would make the kids safe. I didn't think it would, but we were all carrying more weight than we were built for. It wasn't like I knew what would keep them safe. It wasn't like I believed in safety. If he fell back on the familiar, was he any more absurd than Peg and I were in our hesitation? He was young. I know I'm repeating myself, but he was. He had no idea of the ways a simple action can lead to dead fish, or to fire.

I asked Peg if it would do any good to talk with Deena, to ask her to tone things down in front of the kids. If we put it in terms of what was best for the kids, wouldn't she listen to that?

"She might. And it might be like pointing out a sharp knife and saying, 'See that? It will make you powerful and dangerous, so don't touch it.'"

I nodded. I wasn't surprised not to have found the solution. Maybe I was relieved. If it all went wrong, it wouldn't be my doing.

About a week later, Peg got a letter from Deena.

"Listen to this shit," she said.

I listened. It said that Peg and Jude had destroyed Deena as a human being – that was the phrase: "destroyed me as a human being" – and she no longer considered them her sisters. She hoped they wouldn't poison the kids' minds against her but if they did it would turn around and bite them in the ass because the kids knew who their mother was.

Peg tossed the letter down.

"Has she looked at Kerri lately? Does she have even a clue what a kid that age is capable of knowing?"

"She's talking out of her ass. You don't want to think about this too deeply."

"Jesus Christ, though."

She picked the letter up but instead of reading any more she tossed it back down.

"I can't even read this shit."

I pulled it toward me, found the spot where she'd left off, and read it to myself.

"Oh, fuck, go ahead and read it to me," she said. "I'll have to read it sooner or later."

I read it out loud.

Deena couldn't live in a town where she had to see Peg's and Jude's names every time she opened the phone book. They should tell the girls she loved them and thought of them every day. She'd send a photograph so they could remember her.

"Fuck," Peg said, breathing it out slow – like a prayer, like a curse, like an observation on the state of the world.

I waited. This was her sister, not mine. I wasn't sure what to say anyway.

"If the phone book's all she's worried about she might as well stay."

Which was true. Like every other therapist in town, Peg wasn't listed. The phone was in my name. And Jude and Dex's was in his because he was clomping around in his father's shoes, playing I'm-the-head-of-the-household.

Who went through the phone book looking for names she didn't want to see anyway?

We went over the letter again and pulled it to bits, line by line – this was crazy, that was stupid, something else was taking no responsibility for her own part in what happened and this other bit was just plain wrong. We were talking the way people scratch at a mosquito bite, because they can't stand not to.

Neither of us expected her to stay gone. For months, maybe for years, I waited for the 3 a.m. phone calls, for the letters, for the threats. I waited to hear that she'd turned up outside Jude and Dex's, howling for her kids. Somewhere in there, I must've been waiting for the shredded flowers. But she did none of that. She sent a picture for the kids and then she fell off the map.

A few times over the years Peg talked about looking for her – not to make contact, just to make sure she was still alive – but we told each other that someone would have let us know if she wasn't. When my father died, a neighbor tracked me down.

We chose to believe it would have happened that way if Deena'd died, because we were afraid to find out any different; afraid, even though it made no sense, that locating Deena would draw her back before the kids had time to grow up.

So we did nothing, and the kids grew older. Krys collected horse toys, horse pictures, horse anythings, with an intensity that was unnerving, given the promise it grew out of. After the first few days, though, she stopped asking about Deena. Maybe she overheard us talking and didn't need to ask, but maybe something convinced her the subject was off-limits. We should probably have talked to her about Deena so she'd know it was okay, but that's hindsight. We did what we could manage. We were all clunking around in somebody else's shoes. We shaped ourselves around this new gap in our lives and we weren't unchanged or undamaged by it, but you can't ask that from life. Or you can ask, but asking doesn't change anything. We did the only thing people can do in these situations: we went on.

3

As surely as the kids got older, so did we, although we didn't notice it the same way. Time slid past while we were drinking coffee, or tossing our dirty clothes into the washing machine, or walking the kids through the zoo, and it was only once in a while that we noticed a change. I switched to decaf after supper, and then Peg did. We hadn't gone to the bars or a dance in ages, and when the Coffeehouse closed we didn't even hear about it for months. Peg said that if we'd known when we first met how tame we'd become, we'd have run screaming, not from each other but from ourselves. By the time it happened, though, I was happy enough to spend a Saturday night reading or watching TV as long as Peg was in her chair across the room from me. Not ecstatic, not overflowing, but content, although once in a while noticing that I was content was enough to make me overflow. Even then I knew not to take that for granted.

Peg talked about problems at work sometimes – organization problems, coworker problems, client problems – but I understood them as moments, as things that passed, because what job doesn't have its problems? I didn't make the leap from those moments to thinking she was unhappy with what she did.

I can pinpoint the day that changed. She came through the back door with some half a dozen snowflakes resting on her hair, and just before they winked out I had time to think they were beautiful.

"You suppose they'd hire me as a bus driver?" she said before she'd even unzipped her jacket.

I made a small noise that wasn't a real laugh, just an acknowledgment of the joke.

"You'd be wasted."

"Don't be so sure."

Her voice was flat and her mouth tucked back at the corners. She wasn't being even remotely funny, and I had to let myself know this. I opened my mouth to say something but nothing sensible came out. I said "I" and let it fade away, since I had no idea what I'd meant to say next.

Peg pushed her shoes off, the toes of one foot against the heels of the other, one hand on the kitchen counter for balance, then she dropped her jacket and scarf on top of them.

Leave them there, I told myself. *Just fuckin' leave them.*

"I'm not sure how much longer I can go on doing therapy."

Her hand was back on the counter, not for balance now but as if she needed the support.

I heard the words but couldn't catch up with what they meant. Or maybe I wouldn't catch up. Instead I turned away and got water glasses out of the cupboard. Behind me, she opened the refrigerator and bumped things around, making more noise than she needed to, pulling at me to ask what was wrong, but the words had locked up inside me.

I turned the tap on and waited for the water to run cold while Peg bumped more things and clanked other things. She never took well to being ignored. Something clinked onto the microwave floor and the microwave hummed around last night's leftovers. I carried our glasses to the table, still without turning toward Peg, and wiped off an already clean section of counter.

"Can I tell you what happened?" she said over the microwave. "Or don't you want to hear this?"

I turned and nodded: sure, tell me anything. I'm warm and supportive and an all-around good person. I accept you exactly as you are. Nothing awful will happen if you turn bitter and angry and disappointed with the life you worked so hard to build. My stomach clenched itself into a fist and if my ears had been able to do the same thing they would have. I leaned against the table, arms crossed and facing her but letting my eyes slide a few inches to the side, hiding from her about as effectively as a kid covering her eyes and thinking she's invisible. Between us, the length of our small kitchen lay like a no-man's-land – a no-woman's-land – measured out in the cream and brick-red linoleum tiles I'd laid down when we first moved in. I felt the wrongness, the unreceptiveness, of the way I was standing and of where I was standing and I scrambled to rearrange whatever this was that I felt so it would match what I wanted to feel, or what I wanted Peg to believe I felt. I unfolded my arms, but instead of bringing my feelings into line it left me feeling bare and undefended. Noticing the mismatch between words and feelings was what Peg did for a living, and it didn't make her a comfortable person to lie to, although I wouldn't have said right then that I was lying, only that I was trying to hear her out.

Seconds slid past. The hum of the microwave sounded loud enough that I couldn't imagine how we'd talk over it.

"I'm trying to figure out where to start," she said.

I nodded as if I understood. As if I wanted to understand.

"The thing is, we don't know what we're doing," she said.

I nodded.

"We're like doctors were before germ theory. People come to us, we do what we know how to do, and sometimes it even works, but it's all just bumping around in the dark. Whatever we—" She stopped and shook her head as if that was the wrong way into the maze. "Look, I saw a client today. Bright woman. Funny, stubborn, kind of an overage bad girl. You know the type? Been seeing me for months. She reminds me of Deena in a lot of ways. The intensity. The thing is, she cuts on herself and I don't know if it's because she can't stop or because she doesn't want to stop or because I'm a lousy therapist and I can't get her to stop, all I know is we're not getting anywhere. It's not changing. She says it releases the pressure, keeps her from doing anything worse, and hell, I don't know, maybe she's right. I'm not supposed to think that, but maybe while I'm trying to talk her past it there's just some glitch in her brain chemistry, something way past what talk can get to. She had one of those childhoods, you know? Mother pushed her out of a moving car when she was a kid, and – shit, that's just the start of it. Maybe once things like that happen in a kid's life – the brain's still developing, you know?"

She turned aside. The microwave had stopped humming. I couldn't remember hearing it ding.

"I just feel so useless. People come in expecting miracles—"

"You're a good therapist."

Something almost desperate lay under the surface of my words, and I think we both heard it: You *have* to be a good therapist. I can't stand for you *not* to be a good therapist.

"We're none of us good enough."

The silence was louder than the microwave had been. She was looking out the kitchen window and even then, while she was trying to explain the limits of what she could do, it crossed my mind that if she'd only see a therapist herself she'd learn to feel good about however much she could do instead of measuring it against what she couldn't, as if – the real world be damned – therapy was some kind of giant eraser that wiped away the feelings we didn't like, leaving us only the ones we wanted.

I believed that and I didn't believe it.

"Fuck it," she said, pushing herself away from the counter and opening the microwave. "Let's eat."

She'd made a curry the night before, not with curry powder but with half a dozen spices, so that it was hot, with little sweet bits, layer after layer of separate tastes, but it might as well have been canned spaghetti for all I cared right then. Still, we ate, and we looked at our plates as if they were the most interesting things in the house.

"You know what we are good at?" she said a few minutes later, as if no time had passed. "The best of us? Soothing the worried well."

I nodded in a decent imitation of understanding, but if that was all therapists could do, then I wanted her to soothe them and be happy about it. Wasn't it better than driving a bus?

"For a long time I thought if I just learned more I could do it. I thought – I thought somebody out there knew how to fix people. My god, there's a whole industry training therapists, so I thought they had the secrets. The thing is, they don't. No one does. We don't have the answers. For the really hard stuff, nobody fuckin' well knows. The experts just come in, do their workshops, show their videos, collect their fees and then they go someplace else and leave us—"

She waved one hand to finish the sentence. I nodded some more.

"Leave us to struggle with the same old shit and wonder what we're doing wrong when whatever they told us would work doesn't."

I nodded. Outside the window, the snow had gotten heavier. It flickered into the bronze-colored wedge of light under the alley's streetlamp and then flickered out of it, as gentle as love, as thick as despair.

"And I'll tell you what doesn't help," she said.

I turned away from the snow and glanced at her long enough to let her know I was listening, long enough to see that she wasn't even pretending to eat, long enough to admit to myself that she was unsettling something very basic in me.

"What doesn't help is when they act like they've never had a failure and leave us all feeling like shit because we do have them. We have lots of them."

She pushed her plate away. I swallowed a forkful of curry and waited for the fist of my stomach to shift its grip a bit and let it in.

If she couldn't work as a therapist, what would Peg do? I couldn't see her driving a bus – it would be like dreaming in black-and-white when all her life she'd been dreaming in color – but I also couldn't see her plodding on as a therapist after she'd lost her belief in it.

The snow flickered into the light and out of it. Peg turned her head toward the window and her hair swung loose from behind one ear, covering half her face. She pushed it back.

"I'm not going to quit or anything. You don't have to worry."

"You could," I said. "We'd be okay till you figure out what else to do."

That much was true. We could cut back; she could find something temporary; it wouldn't go on forever. I'd worry about money, but I knew how to handle a worry like that.

"We could make it."

"I'll be okay. Other people manage."

She did manage, although every so often one of the failures got to her again and she talked about driving a bus, about working in a coffee shop, and I made myself listen without turning away, even though my stomach knotted itself against the thought that this time she really meant it, this time the world as we knew it really would end. I told her she was good at what she did, and even though I never saw her work I believed I was telling the truth, because I knew who she was and what she carried into those sessions with her clients, even when they failed. I knew that success happens slowly, when you're not around to see it, and that failure follows you down the street pointing a finger and screaming your name. I knew she gave more weight to the failures than to the successes.

I tried to convince her of that once and she said, "You have to."

Sometimes I wondered if the collision of client hopes and therapy's limits crashed as hard into other therapists' lives as it did into Peg's – into ours, really – and mostly I believed that it didn't. Sometimes I thought that was because she cared more than they did, or because she was brighter, so she saw what they either couldn't or didn't let themselves see. Other times I thought she wasn't as good at carrying the weight and I wished she'd just learn to plod through like everybody else, without thinking there had to be something more.

I never said any of that to her. Instead I carried it around, neatly encapsulated in my mind – except of course for the times it leaked out and I got mad at her about something that had nothing to do with it.

It all seems so pointless now. I was mad at Peg for not carrying that impossible weight lightly and there I was, not doing any better with the weight I carried, convinced that Peg's failure to love her work would shatter the contentment we'd found – or that I thought we'd found. Convinced that the danger came from Peg having to live in black-and-white, Peg turning out not to be as good a therapist as I still believe she was. But when the world did end, it wasn't because therapists are like the doctors who worked before germ theory but because the doctors who treat cancer are. They do what they can with the tools they have and it's not enough, and some days I'd like to follow them down the street pointing a finger and yelling their names.

After Peg was diagnosed, I read everything about cancer that I could get my hands on. I read with as much dedication as if I was going to find something the doctors didn't know, or something they knew but wouldn't tell us. I read as if reading would save us. I learned that a tumor of one centimeter can be made up of as many as a billion malignant cells.

By the time we found out about Peg's tumor, it was already made up of six billion cells, or three trillion of them. No one was counting by then. I don't know how much time the cells had had to multiply or, now that I think about it, how big the tumor was. I'm not even sure when the symptoms started. At some point I'd noticed that Peg was in the bathroom a lot, and I knew she'd be embarrassed if I asked about it. When I first got to know Peg, I imagined her as someone who lived her life out in the open, with no silences, no fears, no secrets, but no one lives that way and I'd come to accept that. So I didn't ask, and I congratulated myself for knowing not to. In all the brilliance of hindsight, I could blame myself for not raising the alarm, but I don't really believe I'd have changed anything. With ovarian cancer, by the time you notice that the symptoms are more than isolated quirks your body's developed, the odds are that you're too late. What I regret instead is leaving her alone for weeks with the knowledge that something wasn't right, with the fear that, once she'd told me, the problem would be real.

The time she picked to put words to her fears was when the TV was on and I was more than half lost in the world behind the glass.

"I might as well tell you," she said, and then for a long minute she didn't. I was watching one of those ads that make you think the life you want involves driving through mountains, insulated from the real world by an expensive suspension system and leather seats. I turned away from the screen to look at her, to find out what had happened to the end of the sentence.

"I've been having—"

She tipped her head to one side to mark the hopelessness of approaching whatever this was about from that direction.

"I think I might have colon cancer."

I nodded. A friend's mother had been diagnosed with colon cancer a couple of years before, so we knew the symptoms. We didn't know the recovery rates, but we were working with a sample of one and a hundred percent of it had recovered, thanks.

"I'm having a lot of Marie's symptoms."

I nodded again. I noticed that I was calm, and this seemed like a good thing. It would let me be helpful, encouraging, responsible. We were together. We could get through this.

I said, "It's probably six other things, you know?"

She said it probably was. We agreed that she should go to the doctor, then we told each other how likely it was to be nothing at all, and before the chatter could turn too hollow we refocused on the TV, where the life we wanted now involved walking at the edge of the ocean, splashing our feet through the frill of a wave and fueling our joy with fiber pills.

I turned back to Peg to ask if she was okay and she said she was, she was fine, she felt better now that she'd said something.

. . .

It took her a couple of days to get a doctor's appointment, and endless weeks to make the rounds of the specialists. One after another, they found nothing wrong with their particular subsection of her body.

That was the worst stretch. Every time a specialist found nothing wrong, we started over: a new specialist, a new set of unknowns, a new shape for our fears. Between the time I got off work and the time when Peg did, I sat in the library and read about cancer. It seemed wise to learn what I could. It seemed wise not to tell her what I was doing. Neither of us was sleeping well. We thought we owed it to each other to be brave, so as soon as we turned out the light all the fears we kept muzzled during the day got loose and snapped at us.

One of the doctors decided, finally, to do a laparoscopy – exploratory surgery using a tiny I-don't-know-what: a camera, a miniature submarine, a robot the size of a grain of rice that's controlled from outer space. I never thought to ask what they used, and if it was mentioned in any of the books I read it wasn't what I was looking for so my mind bounced right over it. I took the day off work and drove Peg to the hospital, and after they'd tucked her onto a gurney and draped a blanket over her I rode up in the elevator beside her. She reached through the rails and held my hand and she looked so completely mortal that I understood for the first time that they were going to put a knife into her flesh, and letting them do that struck me as a bigger risk than leaving things alone.

The elevator doors opened and I let myself be shunted off to the waiting room with a collection of people who, as far as I could tell, thought surgery was as simple as getting the oil changed. All they had to do was prove someone would pay and then keep themselves amused while other people did the work. I found an empty chair near a man and a woman in their thirties who were fitting the pieces of a jigsaw puzzle together. They looked like a couple of vacationers killing time on a rainy weekend.

I shifted in my chair for a few minutes, and when I couldn't spend one more second watching them I went out to pace the halls. In a different waiting room I picked up a newspaper someone had left and leaned against a wall to read it, but I couldn't concentrate – the words separated and the meaning leaked out of the gaps between them. I took myself back to the waiting room I belonged in, settled into a chair well away from the people with the jigsaw puzzle, and stared out the window at the green-gold mix of fall leaves. Enough time passed for the earth's tectonic plates to make every map I'd ever seen obsolete, although judging by the leaves outside it still seemed to be fall.

Finally a nurse called me in to sit with Peg in the recovery room. She was lying on, as far as I could tell, the same gurney with the rails still up.

"How you doing?" I said.

She smiled at me, hazy-eyed and full of drugs, and didn't seem to remember that the correct response to a question was an answer.

I held her hand. More time passed. The doctor came in. He moved like an actor or a dancer, like the kind of man who draws your eyes whether you're interested in him or not. I thought what an odd thing it was to care about right then. I had the sense that I was clearing space in my head for whatever he had to say, being careful not to pour anything into it myself. It was a kind of superstition: if I keep this space empty, no bad news will fill it.

"Well, we had a look around," he said.

He was looking at Peg but his eyes flicked toward me just long enough to acknowledge that I was part of his audience, and I sat in perfect emptiness, waiting for whatever came next. Peg smiled at him, stoned serenely out of her mind.

He told us about ovaries and tumors, about the metastatic process and the difference between ameliorating the symptoms and aggressive treatment. He told us about the odds of success if they did this or that or seven other things. He cited statistics. And all the while, Peg smiled, not taking in a fucking word. I couldn't break in to ask questions because what seemed to matter most was that Peg keep smiling. I was still holding her hand, although I don't think she remembered that she had a hand right then. It had a vacant quality to it, as if she'd slipped away and left me snuggled up with an old sock. I wanted to take my hand back but was afraid of making her notice that something was wrong.

It's not that I wanted to keep the truth from her, but I could no more have been the cause of her finding out right then than I could have taken the pillow from under her head and smothered her.

Peg pulled her hand out of mine and hauled herself upright, all hazy and smiling even harder, and she started telling the doctor how much she appreciated, but before she got as far as saying what she appreciated she threw up. I was grateful for a reason to turn away, to run for a towel, to get swept aside by the nurse.

By the time Peg was cleaned up, the doctor had gone, almost as if he'd never been there.

Once a tumor is established it sends out clusters of cells, which act like missionaries. Their job is to convert the pagan hordes. Most of the missionaries die. The environment they land in is too foreign. Cells from an ovary land in the liver, where they don't speak the language, but they're good observers and notice that the liver cells divide in ways the missionary cells find offensive. The missionary cells pine away in isolation. Or else the liver cells look deep into the theological convolutions of the missionary DNA, don't like what they see there, and do their best to slaughter them. Better for everyone, they say. Kinder in the long run.

But malignant cells divide quickly. The tumor has cells to spare, and it sends out more, and more again. And some of them survive. They found mission societies, study foreign languages, build churches and schools where they sing hymns and call on their god for strength.

By the time we learned about it, Peg's cancer was as well established as the Catholic Church before Martin Luther bought himself that first hammer.

I offered to go with Peg to her first doctor's appointment after the laparoscopy, but she said I'd missed enough work, she'd be fine, and I couldn't tell her that she wouldn't be. Whatever drugs had left her smiling had long since worn off but I was hostage to the memory that she had, for a flash-bulb's measure of time, been perfectly happy.

That's not entirely true. I don't know why I couldn't tell her. Because I thought it would buy us some time. Because I didn't want it to be true. Because I was afraid of the pain the words would cause me. I grab hold of explanations, but what good does it do to have an explanation anyway? The act was the same, whatever my reason was.

I don't know how Peg got through the time between her appointment and me coming home from work, but when I walked in the back door she was sitting at the kitchen table with a solitaire game laid out in front of her – one of those multilayered ones where you deal out all the cards at the beginning and the chances of winning are almost zero. She'd never liked card games, but maybe it soothed her to see the odds against her laid out so clearly, to lose at something where the stakes were so low.

She looked up at me, then back at the table so she could lay the cards she was holding on a new row. The deck was an old one and the cards made a slushy sound when she laid them down.

"I'm already dead," she said.

"I know."

I was afraid she'd ask how I knew and why I hadn't told her. I was afraid I'd have to account for elements of my behavior that made no sense to me, afraid that nothing I could say would be enough to justify them. It was one of my beliefs that I shouldn't keep secrets from her, or at least that she shouldn't know I was keeping secrets. I would have traded my cancer-free insides for her missionary-ridden ones on the spot if there'd been a way, but doing something as simple as explaining why I hadn't told her what I knew – that was beyond me. I was sure we'd be drawn into one of those naggy little clusters of understandings and misunderstandings and hurt feelings that could still, sometimes, leave us both miserable for hours.

She didn't ask, though. She looked back at her cards and I thought she was looking for her next move but after a few seconds she swept them into a heap, face up and face down all slushed in together.

"When I heard him talking in the hospital," she said, "there were all these numbers involved. I'm not sure what I thought he said, but it seemed like as long as there were numbers involved I was okay."

She picked a handful of cards off the pile and turned them so they faced up, then she pushed them into the heap of scrambled ones. I wanted to kneel beside her, I wanted to touch her, but I let myself get snagged by the mechanics of how I'd fit into the space between her chair and the recycling bins. And I was afraid of the moment when we'd start to cry.

"We should check our wills," she said. "Make sure they're okay. Or I should. I don't suppose you have to."

"We might as well both."

As if my participation could shield her.

She looked back to the cards and spread them apart so she could flip them all face down.

"I'll work as long as I can," she said to the cards.

"You don't have to, you know."

We'd been saving money to retire on, and I felt the bitterness of that joke register behind my nose and breathe itself out in a narrow stream of air. Christ, the plans we'd made and unmade and argued over. I wanted that money gone now, spent on what was left of Peg's life so that once she died I wouldn't think I'd held anything back from her.

"I can't just sit around the house waiting to die."

"We'll both quit. We'll rent a camper and drive out west or something. See the national parks. Put our feet in the ocean."

It was an image from that ad: the two of us walking along the beach, kicking up a fine spray of salt water.

"Fuck the ocean."

I laughed. And then I went ahead and cried, as if the one naturally triggered the other, and she got out of her chair, still moving like spun glass after her surgery, and held me as if I was the one who was dying.

I sobbed the way the kids had sobbed when they were little,

holding nothing back. I wept until I was empty, and then we sat at the kitchen table and talked, in a peculiarly rational and shell-shocked way, about who to call and how to tell the kids. We talked about whether chemotherapy made any sense, and I wanted her to have it even though I understood that it was too late and that she'd already decided not to. Anything to let me think we had some choices left to make.

And then, as if I'd admitted that we didn't, we talked about funerals.

"Don't let them sell you a bunch of shit, okay? I don't even want a fuckin' casket. Just stick me in a paper bag if they need something to put me in. I don't want those vultures getting one more goddamn dime than they have to. I'd rather have you cremate the money alongside me than give it to them."

I promised I wouldn't let them sell me a bunch of shit. If she'd asked me to make her a coffin out of matchsticks and set it on fire in the backyard, I'd have promised.

"I hate to leave you," she said.

I cried all over again.

We went back to work. Both of us. It was what we knew how to do. Peg told Jude and Dex and the kids. She told her boss, her clients, her friends, her coworkers. She waded through their feelings and then back through her own until she'd been scoured clean and the first wind that came along could have blown straight through her.

I told no one. I didn't want sympathy. I didn't want to answer questions or feel people weighing my grief.

I didn't want, I think now, to weigh my own grief.

At home, I found small jobs that needed doing, jobs I'd managed not to do for years. The knobs on the kitchen cupboards were loose and I pulled them all off and replaced the screws with longer ones. I shampooed rugs and oiled hinges and fixed drips. I took the living-room curtains down and shredded them on the gentle cycle. These were the curtains Peg had owned when I first met her, the curtains that had hung in that incense-soaked, non-parlor apartment where we'd first lain together, skin against skin, and where I'd first learned to love her. When I went to hang them over the line in the basement – I was so pleased with myself for knowing not to put them in the dryer – and saw what I'd done I stood on the cement floor and wept all over again. Then I straightened the first panel so it would dry without wrinkles and I hung the second one beside it. I had a sense – it wasn't clear enough to be a thought – that somebody somewhere would know how to reconnect the broken threads and piece the pattern back together. I also knew this wasn't possible. The two beliefs lived side by side for a second, then the first one flickered out and I was left with damp hands and a runny nose and no way to tell Peg what I'd done. Because even then, when we both knew she was dying and we were almost without walls, my first thought was about how to protect myself. From what? From the faintest hint of a possibility of blame. As if even then what mattered most in the world was that nothing be my fault. I stood in front of the clothesline not so much wondering what to say as flailing around for an excuse I could believe in.

In the end, I took the curtains upstairs, where Peg lay stretched on the couch, and unfurled one panel as carefully as if care would make a difference.

"I didn't know they were so fragile," I said, more or less blaming the curtains. "I am so sorry."

I was getting ready to cry again. If I'd gotten as far as saying "I know you loved them", I would have.

It's odd how much easier it was to cry over the curtains than over Peg herself.

"It doesn't matter," she said.

"But you loved them."

The balance had shifted now and the words were safe.

"They're just stuff."

They were just stuff, but if she was ready to leave it all behind, I wasn't. They were her stuff and I couldn't make myself not care about them. I took them back downstairs and hung them back over the line, spreading them out to dry neatly, and when they did I folded them and stored them in the back of my closet as if they were something I'd be able to use someday.

I kept meaning to replace them, but Peg had found them in a second-hand store for five dollars, and they were cotton and soft to the touch. I didn't know curtains or cottons or what a fair price would be all these years later. I didn't know antique from rummage sale. I couldn't expect to find those exact curtains waiting for me on a shelf somewhere, and I couldn't imagine accepting anything else. So I put off looking. I kept thinking Peg might go curtain hunting with me, but she was hoarding her energy by then. What did curtains matter to her? She was dying. When she had the strength, we went to a movie or we saw friends. We went to supper at Jude and Dex's and the smell of food when we walked in the door made her sick. She told us to eat without her and she lay on the couch with the window open.

The rest of us put our heads down and shoveled our food as if someone had rigged it with a timer and it would explode if we didn't get it down fast. Twice I went in to see how she was. The first time she lay on her side facing the back of the couch, and she talked to me without turning. The second time she was facing into the room and that seemed like an improvement. By the time we'd dumped the leftovers into refrigerator dishes and washed away the food smells, she was sitting up with her legs stretched halfway down the couch.

She was at her best that night, telling the kids she'd thrown up on the surgeon and provoking them until they told vomit stories of their own. Any other time Jude would have jumped all over them for that but they got a free pass that night, and they made the most of it.

In an odd way, those months when Peg was dying were some of the best time we had together. We'd always been closest when the world was crashing down around us. When I thought about what would happen next I was sure I couldn't face it, but the changes came one at a time, and with each one I could take hold of myself, tell myself not to turn away, and I didn't. Or I did, but then I turned back. What choice was there? I learned to massage her legs when the pain was bad, not because it made the pain go away but because the distraction sometimes helped, and because it was something I could do for her. I learned to love her all over again. Not the way I had that first night, when she'd let the phone ring. I wasn't reaching for anything now beyond the touch of her skin on my hand. All I wanted was that moment, the two of us, her skin and mine, the world narrowed down to something that small – something that wasn't sex but was at least as powerful. Later, when her legs were puffed with liquid and the skin was dry and thin, I traced the bony length of her fingers and the tendons hidden under her palms. If I could have done that forever, I would have considered myself happy.

It was around this time that she started planning her funeral. She didn't want me to have to do that, she said, she knew I hated that kind of thing, and I listened to her and thought, *I do?*, half of me convinced she was wrong and the other half sure she knew more about me than I did.

Maybe she took some comfort from the planning, because she planned enough send-offs to cover all the victims of a mid-sized natural disaster, working her way through funerals, memorial meetings, gatherings at our house and at friends' houses, not liking the informality of the one, the money the vultures would make off the next, the finality of them all.

At the end we were overrun with helpers – friends, hospice volunteers, a visiting nurse, Jude. Even the kids took shifts. I was grateful to them all and I hated having them in our house. They tracked grit in on their shoes or else they lined their shoes up inside the door and shooshed around too respectfully in their socks. They brought articles about people who'd been cured of cancer by meditation, or by eating garlic or deep-fried cheese curds and pork, or by ingesting nothing but sunlight and the purest of filtered water. They either ran the vacuum or didn't run the vacuum. They made too much noise or were too quiet, with their lowered voices and sick-room footsteps. I don't know what we'd have done without them but they were every one of them going to go on living after Peg was dead, and I could see that with every step they took. There were moments when I hated them for it, and they were kind enough not to notice.

It was Jude, finally, who replaced the curtains. It was a Sunday, not long before the end, and she'd come over so I could go out and buy groceries. I was eating frozen things that came in plastic trays by then. I'd gotten in the habit when the smell of food first started making Peg sick, because they didn't smell so much like food, since they were only loosely related to it. Besides, I hadn't cooked in years.

I came in with my grocery bags, letting a gust of cold spring wind through the kitchen door, and found Jude standing on a chair beside the living-room window, wrestling one side of the rust-flecked curtain rod back onto its bracket. She didn't turn until she had it in place.

"She's asleep," she whispered, nodding toward the stairs in case I wasn't sure who she meant. She climbed off the chair and twitched the curtains into place.

Peg slept most of the time by then. We whispered out of habit, not because we were likely to wake her.

"What's with these?"

I pointed at the curtains. They were harsh white, and stiff, as if they'd been spun out of old plastic pill bottles.

"I thought, the bare windows – you know. Depressing."

I should have smiled. I should have said they were great, they were wonderful, they were gorgeous. At the very least I should have said they were thoughtful, or that she was. I knew all of that and my face seemed to be wearing one of those lead aprons that dentists spread over you before they take X-rays. I wasn't strong enough to lift its weight.

"I kept meaning to look—" I said.

It was the best I could do, and she seemed to hear a version of thanks in it, because she went off into a speech about my responsibilities, my time, and all the things Peg and I had done when the kids were small, how Peg was the only sister she had left and she just wanted to do something but she felt so helpless.

I hugged her and she shut up and hugged me back, and I still hated the curtains but I was grateful beyond the reach of words for what she'd meant to do.

When she'd gone home, I stacked my prefabricated slabs of sustenance in the freezer and folded away the grocery bags, and then there was nothing left to do but stand in the doorway to the living room staring at the curtains. This was what my life would be like without Peg. All the things that had softened it would wear out, or die out, or dry up and blow away, and if I replaced them at all, or if someone else did, it would be with things that were nothing like what I'd had before.

I went upstairs and sat on the floor beside the bed to watch Peg sleep while I still could. Her mouth was closed and each time she blew a breath out her lips made a sound like the cork popping off a tadpole's champagne bottle – a tiny, improbable celebration that life was still going on here, even if it was only for the space of one more breath.

A few days before she died, and a long time, in the slow way I measured time then, after she'd stopped worrying about funerals, Peg said, as if we'd just been talking about it, "You remember what I wanted for the funeral?"

She wasn't whispering but her voice had a whispery quality, as if she couldn't wake herself up all the way.

I said sure, not wanting to ask which of the plans I was supposed to be remembering.

"I decided not to die, so don't bother."

I told her that sounded good and we both smiled. I have no way of knowing whether her mind was clear enough for it to have been a joke.

And then she did die, and Jude and I picked through as many of the plans as I remembered, looking for the elements she'd mentioned most often, for the bits that struck us as most Peg-like, and we patched something together from that. Jude couldn't accept the idea of a memorial meeting, and since *funeral* had been Peg's last word on the subject I was able to convince myself that it was okay, even though it gave a massive chunk of money to the vultures. It didn't matter, really, what Peg had wanted. She was dead, Jude was alive and full of feelings, and I didn't much care right then what we did.

The kids came to the funeral, looking self-important and touching in their sober new clothes and their raw sadness, and they were the only people who did touch me that day – the way they looked impressed by this irrevocable, adult thing that had happened to them. Jake's chin trembled when he came over to talk with me, and he turned away, and I pretended I hadn't noticed until he fought it down and turned back to nod and, of all things, shake my hand. I squeezed his fingers, thinking that this was the point of all the ceremony and silliness, this tiny moment when someone tries to say, You're not alone. All the planning, all the stage sets and the props and the costumes – they're all there so that this one thing can happen.

But formalities end. Sooner or later, you go home. And you are alone.

4

BEFORE Peg got sick I thought of memory as the quick stab of regret. I'd catch a fleeting image of the staircase to Peg's old apartment – something I hadn't even known I was recording when I pounded down it after Megan. Or, the same way you feel a bass drum inside your belly, I'd feel the sound that a human body makes smashing into a dumpster. That was memory: a string of moments I'd never be free of.

Now memory is all that matters. Images of Peg appear in my mind like slides projected on a blank wall, all light and no substance, pictures I can see but not hold, that I can't call for and can't keep. I've seen her head burrowed deep into her pillow and turned away from me, the covers pulled to her neck so that all I saw of her was hair, one ear, the fingers of her left hand curled above the blanket on her right shoulder, and before I had time to want more, even that much of her was gone. I've seen her with Kerri riding one hip, Kerri's hand pulling Peg's T-shirt askew, the two of them touching and me unable to brush so much as a finger across them.

I lie on the couch and watch the light shift across the far wall, or I watch TV, and the images come to me when they will. The phone rings. Old friends call, and I say that I'm okay, that I appreciate the call, that I don't want to do anything, go anywhere, see anyone.

I work, I come home, I watch the light shift across the wall. I sign up for overtime when it's available. If it weren't for the days of the week printed in the newspaper I'd forget when to go to work and when to stay home.

I remember how Peg used to sit on the edge of the bed to clip her toenails, letting the cuttings spray onto the rug, and sometimes onto the sheet, and how mad I used to get at her about that, year after year, as if I still thought I could change her, as if she'd be a better person if I could, as if brushing the occasional nail clipping out of bed was more of a burden than I could bear. I remember this and I can't call her back and do it better this time around, or even tell her how sorry I am, and time passes the way it does when you're in physical pain, slowly but without markers, so that it's hard to tell two hours from twelve.

I'm in my usual spot, flattened on the couch and staring at the dining-room wall, thinking about the things I could do if I once managed to set myself upright and move to some other place – the kitchen, maybe, or the dining room, which has turned into a warehouse for all the things I don't care about enough to put away. People have stopped calling, mostly, so when the phone rings the sound makes me jump. I've missed the calls and I'm annoyed to have one. I think about letting the machine pick up, but even while I'm thinking it I'm already hauling myself off the couch.

Jude's voice comes out of the phone, scattering apologies. She doesn't like to bother me with her troubles, she knows how it is right now.

No, I think. *You don't know. May you never know.* But there's no anger behind the thought. There's no passion of any kind. It floats past me like a fleck of dust in a sunbeam – it's there, I watch it, and it's gone. Or else, it's still there but I've looked away, so it might as well be gone.

"The thing is, is it's Krys," she says.

Krys. New fleck of dust, same old sunbeam. Of course it's Krys. If it was going to be anyone, it was going to be Krys.

Jude waits for an invitation to go on, so I give it.

"What about her?"

"She hasn't called, has she?"

"What about?"

She's been gone since Monday, Jude says. I have to think a minute before I can locate myself in the week. Wednesday. Today is Wednesday.

"The thing of it is, is I know where she's been – it's not like somebody's kidnapped her or anything – I just don't know where she is now. I mean, I've called everybody."

I say, "Shit." I say, "Fuck." I say all the other words I can think of for punctuation, even though Jude hates hearing them, and I carry the phone to the back door, where I can rest my forehead against the glass to feel the cold spread across my skin and into the bone. I picture Krys outside somewhere. The thermometer Peg nailed to the garage the first summer we owned the house reads sixty degrees. I can't see the needle in the dark, but it won't have changed: all winter it's registered sixty degrees, like one of those mythical clocks that stop when its owner dies. Sixty degrees in tropical Minnesota. I haven't had the heart to look for a new thermometer. It would be the curtains all over again. The details don't matter anyway. It's cold. Somewhere below zero. How much more do I need to know?

"So I just thought, you know, if she does call—"

I cut in to say, "Of course," and then wonder what she'd have said if I hadn't interrupted.

"The thing of it is," Jude says. "What set it all off—"

She waits again and I make a noise – I'm here; I'm listening – so she can go on.

"Oh, hell, I hate to even talk about it. It's Deena all over again is what it is."

"She's pregnant?"

"She most certainly is."

I do a little subtraction and figure she's either sixteen or seventeen. It's hard to keep track of the kids' ages. They keep changing.

"It could be worse," I say. I'm thinking of AIDS, of death,

of dismemberment, either physical or emotional, but even so it's a stupid thing to say. Still, having committed myself to the idea, I try to justify it.

"I mean, she will get older. It's the one thing we can count on."

"That never helped Deena much."

"She could be fourteen. She could have shot half the kids in the school lunchroom."

Jude says, "I suppose that's true," then erases it by saying, "You don't know what it's like."

Which is also true. I don't.

"You should hear Dex on the subject," she says.

"Not happy, huh?"

"I'll tell you about it one of these days."

I ask if there's anything I can do and she says just call if I hear from Krys, just let her know, and I promise twice more before she lets me go.

I hit the phone's off button and imagine Krys calling me now that the line's free. I rehearse what she'll say, and what I'll say, and I lose myself in the conversation even though she's too old to call me, and she's too young, and she's way too pissed off to look for help inside the family.

If I am still family. I don't know where I fit in the kids' world now that Peg's gone. Jude invited me over for supper a few times, and I made myself go, but it was awkward without Peg.

With the phone silent in my hand, I stand at the door, forehead resting on the glass, looking out into the dark. I think about making my way back to the couch and flipping through the channels until I find something to dull the ache but I don't move, even though standing at the door doesn't seem like something a person can do forever. I should make plans. I should at least park myself someplace sensible.

And still I don't move.

When my forehead's ready to shatter with cold, I carry the phone back to its base, but instead of making my way to the couch I put on my jacket, my boots, my knit cap, my gloves. I wind Peg's scarf around my neck, walk out the back door and turn left in the alley. Not because I think Krys is out there for me to find but because I *believe* she is. This is the scenery I was looking at when I heard she was gone and this is where I'm convinced I can find her. It feels true, even though feeling and belief prove nothing more than their own existence. I believed that Peg and I had years left to be together. If belief were information about the world, she'd be out here in the cold with me, moving toward the toxic-looking orange spill of the streetlight, searching the blue-white shadows in the snow where a pregnant teenager just might be hiding if this were a different life, another planet.

As if I'm looking for a lost cat, I think, but I keep looking anyway.

The moon's full, or close enough to it that I can't tell the difference. I cross 35th Street and head down the alley toward Lake. I know bus drivers who swear that people get crazier when the moon's full. They've seen it, they say – more incidents, crazier incidents, right there in front of them. I've never noticed it, but maybe I haven't kept track. Maybe it's the moon that's pushing me into the cold, making me want to pound a fork against a cat food can and call, "Here, kitty, kitty, kitty. Here, kitty."

On the other hand, maybe drivers who think the moon makes us crazy only keep track of the incidents that prove what they believe. Whatever doesn't fit the pattern turns invisible.

I cross Lake Street and stop at a coffee shop I never go to because it's full of sullen teenagers – or people who were teenagers two days ago even if they're technically not anymore. I expect the place to fall silent and everyone to stare at me when I open the door, since I look like what I more or less am – someone's relative, bad news from home, the kind of thing they want desperately to pretend is no part of their lives – but no one even looks up.

I could turn and leave, but instead I step to the counter and buy a decaf to go. It's less awkward to pretend I came in for coffee than to turn around and walk out. The boy behind the counter doesn't put a cardboard sleeve on the cup, making me think that they don't sell much actual coffee, that the kids are young enough to get their caffeine from pop. I pull my gloves back on for insulation.

Outside, I stop and take a sip, even though just the thought of coffee makes my stomach sour. What the hell, I bought the stuff. Even if no one else is keeping track of what I'm doing, I am. I want to think I'm behaving rationally.

The coffee's thin and bitter, though, and as soon as I'm out of sight of the coffee shop I pour it on a snowbank, leaving a brown stain behind. This is Peg's legacy: that I notice the taste; that I care about it; that I'm out here looking for her niece, even if I'm looking in all the wrong places.

By the time I was Krys's age I'd left home twice already. The first time I didn't go any further than a friend's house and after a couple of days her mother decided it was time for me to go eat at home. The second time, I left town with a boy I'd just met and I stayed gone for months. My father took me back after that but he stopped talking to me – wouldn't say "Good morning", "You're an asshole", or anything else. The third time, I figured there was no going back. I saved money, I left a note and I left town. That part of my life was over.

Krys would probably go to a friend's this first time too. If she's out in the cold, it's only until someone's mother goes to bed or someone else's father leaves for work so she can sneak in a basement window. She's okay – or I believe she's okay, for whatever my belief is worth – but even so I'm afraid for her in a way I wasn't for myself. I was so young when I left home that I had only the vaguest idea of what was worth being afraid of.

I walk another ten blocks holding the empty cup crumpled in my hand and looking for Krys – or pretending to look for her – before I'm cold enough to turn toward home.

On Sunday Jude calls to say Krys is back. She'd been sneaking in during the day to grab some food, to take a bath, to stuff her dirty clothes in the bottom of the laundry basket and take some clean ones, dropping a wet towel on the bathroom floor along the way. Hey, who'd notice a wet towel, a little stray laundry? Jude took Friday off and waited for her as if they were playing tag and all she had to do was say, "You're it."

Maybe all Krys wanted was to know Jude would take a day off.

I can't imagine I'd have gone home if my father had come after me, and I can't remember what I did about clothes that first time. I know it didn't involve sneaking into my father's house. There was nothing in that house that I wanted.

Or if I did want something, I've forgotten it. Maybe I've remembered myself into someone fiercer than I really was, someone more independent, someone I like better.

Maybe that's for the best.

So Krys is home again, Jude says, fighting with Dex and tormenting the younger kids.

"I'm telling you," she says, "I slept better not knowing where she was. I'm almost ready to send her back out there."

I'm at the kitchen door again, looking into the dark, although now that I know Krys is home I don't lean my head against the glass to remind myself how cold it is.

"You want her to stay here?" I ask.

This isn't something I've been thinking about. The words come out of my mouth and I hear them as if they were someone else's suggestion. It sounds like a lot of bother but it makes sense, unfortunately.

For half a second, Jude's struck dumb.

"You serious?" she says when words come back.

"Jude, I'm lonely."

I want to pretty that up but I don't have much to work with. I am lonely.

"Do you have any idea what you're getting into?"

"When did I ever?"

Jude laughs, although she only knows the roughest outlines of my life. She understands that I've made a joke and that she owes me a laugh, but she doesn't owe me understanding and if she did she couldn't pay. Peg was the listener in the family, and I miss what she gave me as sharply as if Jude had yanked it out of my hand just this minute.

After the laugh, Jude goes silent on me. She doesn't want to leap at the offer. She doesn't want to be seen to leap at it. On the other hand, she doesn't want it to drift out of reach.

"Let me talk to her," she says.

It must be one hell of a talk, because by the time Jude calls back, it's late. At least, by my standards it's late. We agree that everyone will survive if Krys stays home another night, then she gives me a crash course on prenatal vitamins and doctor's appointments and the possibility of morning sickness, which seems to have stopped but just in case—

A few years back I read an article on preeclampsia, and images from the article come roaring back at me so that by the time I hang up I'm terrified.

When I answer the doorbell the next evening it's Dex that I see first, planted outside the porch door with a nylon gym bag in one hand and a clutch of plastic grocery bags in the other. Only when he starts inside do I see Krys, with a backpack drooping off one shoulder and a pillow clutched to her chest. She waits for me to say "Come on in" before she follows him.

Even now, when she's pregnant and wearing a winter jacket, Krys is all angles and sharp edges. Nothing shows yet. She wears her hair pulled into a network of skinny braids, which lie so tight against her skull that the scalp shows bare and painful-looking between them. I know it's not fair to carve up the ways people can be in the world and assign them to the kids in the family – this is the difficult child, this is the smart one, this one is Aunt Sadie all over again, and that one will drive us to the doctor when we're old – but still we all do it. You live long enough, you begin to see patterns. Or you think you do. Krys is the kid I worry about. She's the kid I understand best: the restless one, the one who wants something she can't find at home. She's the one who can do the most damage and the one who gets hurt most easily, not because she can't fight for herself but because the way she fights signals so clearly where she's vulnerable. All that anger, and instead of protecting her it makes her shatteringly vulnerable.

The three of us pile up in the hallway, not sure whether to go sit in the living room and what to do with our arms if we don't. Dex sets down his collection of bags.

"Well, there you go," he says. "That'll keep you a day or two."

Krys leaves her face in neutral, as if he were talking on the phone to some alleged great-aunt she's never met. He shoves a hand into his pocket, comes out with his key ring, and tosses it in his palm. They had a fight in the car, I decide.

"You'll be okay?" he says to me.

"We'll be fine."

He tosses the key ring.

"If you need anything—"

This is aimed at me still, not at Krys – he's not making her any open-ended offers – but even so I feel like a guest who doesn't have the sense to leave when the family starts arguing. I tell him again that we'll be fine and we run through a few more awkward reassurances. He tosses the keys inside in the cage of his hand, then turns to Krys.

"Remember, you're not living at home now," he tells Krys. "Marge isn't your blood relative and she doesn't have to put up with your crap, so behave yourself."

If I'd drawn up a list of things we don't say to each other, "Marge isn't your blood relative" wouldn't have been on it, but only because I couldn't have imagined anyone saying it out loud. I think it often enough, but that's not the same. The words leave me speechless, but Krys and Dex are too busy trying to stare each other down to notice. I'd have to crash to the floor before I could claim a slice of their attention. They hold their stares for another few long seconds, then Dex tosses his keys one last time and turns toward the door.

Krys waits till he's halfway through.

"You not my blood relative either," she mumbles toward his back.

"I mean it," he says, turning back to take a step toward her. She doesn't back away but she compresses a little and takes up less space. He'd never hit the kids, but he's not above threatening.

I insert myself between him and Krys. Dex has filled out in the years I've known him, and he knows how to use his size, but I'm no smaller than he is and I'm not so much older that it's turned into a disadvantage. Or if it has, we haven't demonstrated it yet. I have an uncomfortable sense that I'm being drawn into some weird kind of male moment with him. Any second now we'll charge at each other and whack our horns together.

"You're letting the heat out," I say.

He looks at the open door as if he'd never heard that doors do that and he pushes it closed.

"I appreciate what you're doing," he says. A formal announcement. Something he meant to say anyway, even if it has to land in this odd spot.

"Not a problem."

We nod at each other a couple of times and try to act as if nothing's happened – no shift in my bulk or his, no possibility of whacking our heads against each other – then he opens the door again and walks through it. I watch him halfway to the sidewalk before I flip off the porch light.

When I turn back to Krys, she's slumped against the wall as if pissing off Dex was the only thing holding her upright. She's still hugging her pillow and she looks out of place and very young, as if she thinks that here, too, she might have to wait till I'm asleep so she can climb in a basement window. I wish she were even younger so I could put a hand on her shoulder or touch her tightly braided hair. It's the only language I trust right now, but you can't do that with teenagers. Maybe that's why they turn angry: we take that away from them.

"Look," I say. "Neither one of us has done this before. We'll have to make it up as we go along, okay?"

She nods.

"I can only think of two things I want: you eat what you want here – don't ask if it's okay, and let me know what you want from the store – and if you're going to be late let me know so I won't think you've been slaughtered somewhere."

She nods.

"Plus whatever your mother – I don't know. She's worried about the vitamins. And the doctor's appointment. You need me to nag you?"

"Nah."

One syllable, barely a word, but it lifts enough that for a second we're having a conversation.

"Anything you want?" I say.

She shrugs.

"Okay, let me know when there is."

She shrugs again.

"Let's make room in the closet for your stuff."

She follows me upstairs, bringing the pillow.

In Peg's closet, everything's still where she left it – the shoes paired up on the floor, the shirts heartbreaking and thin on their wire hangers.

"It's Peg's stuff," I say, nodding toward the closet. "I keep trying to do something with it and I can't."

"I don't need a closet. I'm a slob anyway. Kerri's always complaining about my junk on the floor."

The voice is spring-loaded, impossibly upbeat, as if she'd do anything to have me like her. It makes me realize how flat she sounded with Dex.

"Peg's dead," I say. "She's not coming back."

She looks at the floor as if I'd just told her something about sex that she'd have been happier not learning from me.

"It's okay," I say, meaning I have no idea what since it's not okay and I didn't mean to pretend that it was.

I strip an armload of shirts off their hangers.

"Fold these for me, will you?"

She carries them to the bed and smooths one out as if she expects to find a trace of Peg left in the weave, and I think I could forgive this kid any kind of trouble she causes me. I strip off a few more shirts so she'll have enough to stay busy with and I carry Peg's jacket to my closet and hang it there. She doesn't ask why and I don't explain. Peg *is* dead, someone else could use her jacket, and I don't care. I want to see it when I open my closet door. I want to touch its sleeve, take the woody kleenex out of its pocket, then tuck it back where I know it'll be safe. And I don't want to talk about it. I clump downstairs for the roll of black plastic bags I keep in the cupboard under the sink and I flap one open for Peg's shoes.

"I don't suppose you wear a seven-and-a-half, do you?"

"I think Kerri still might."

I nod, although I'm not agreeing. I could give the shoes to Krys if they fit her. I could see them lined up by my front door again, or tracking snow onto the kitchen floor. I could even be glad of it, in a stab-a-long-piece-of-copper-wire-through-my-heart kind of way. But I'm not ready to hand them to Kerri so she can track snow through Jude's house and then throw them out when they're too small.

I tear off a second bag and whisk it through the air to open it, and I nestle the shirts Krys has folded into the bottom. She's working on the last of the ones I took out. I point to the closet.

"Fold anything you find in there, okay?"

I carry the bag with the shoes to the front porch and settle it into an icy corner. When I get back upstairs, Krys has pulled one of Peg's shirts on and is folding the front panels across her belly to test how much is left once she's accounted for herself and the baby I still can't see a trace of. She looks lost in it.

"Kind of big."

"It's just that most of my stuff – I can't zip my pants anymore."

"Keep it. She'd have been pleased."

It's odd, hearing myself talk as if I had a direct line to Peg. As if she were my only guide to the world. But she would have been pleased, I think, in the same unhappy sort of way that I am.

"You know what Dex is all mad about, don't you," she says.

Dex. Not "my dad" but Dex, that guy passing himself off as my father.

The answer in my mind is, *That you're pregnant*, but I choke on it.

"The baby," I say.

I hadn't known I was such a prude.

"It's Deena," she says. "He's never going to forgive Deena."

I nod as if this was a simple statement, something you could agree with or not instead of separating it into layers, saying, Keep this thought. Pitch that. I'm not sure about the others.

"It's not as if I'd – you know. Do what she did."

"What about Jude?" I ask. "How's she taking it?"

"She's okay. I mean, she's mad at me and all, but she's okay."

I should say something here but I have no idea what. My eyes travel to the closet.

"Take anything you'd use," I say. "I'd rather see you wear it than strangers. I'll leave the bags here for you to go through."

We bag clothes until the closet and chest of drawers are empty, and I don't feel any lonelier than I did this morning, when they were full, although this lack of loss feels like a loss of its own, as if I'm less of a person than I thought I was – less constant, less capable of love.

"I'll get you some sheets and blankets," I say. "Then I've got to get some sleep."

. . .

I drive my route the next morning fretting about food: the kind of food I eat, the kind of food Krys eats, the kind of food the baby needs Krys to eat. I could write everything I know about pregnancy on the inside cover of a matchbook, but I do know she needs to eat.

I should probably worry about some of the larger questions, but food is all I can get my head around. If we pour the right food in, we'll have time to figure the rest out later. So I stop at Rainbow on my way home, yanking a cart out of the chain in the entryway and pushing it through the aisles, past the fruits and vegetables to the meat cooler. Long-forgotten connections fire in my mind and sputter out a grocery list. If pot roast, then potatoes. If potatoes, then an onion. If an onion, then carrots. Sputt, sputt. I tear a plastic bag off the roll and slip it over a chuck roast, keeping two layers of plastic film and a Styrofoam tray between me and the blood leaking out of this thing. Then I backtrack and stall out in front of the vegetables, staring at yellow onions, white onions, red onions, single onions, bagged onions. I haven't bought this kind of food since I left my father's house that last time, but now that I'm here my father and grandmother are both in my head screaming for me to buy bulk. Buy cheap. And normally I'd agree but I can't commit to anything more than this one meal, this one aberration in the way I live. Krys could move home tomorrow and what would I do with all the onions? I pick up a single, overpriced onion the size of a softball, weighing it in my hand as if I am about to pitch it, and I place it in the seat of my cart where Krys's baby would ride if she'd already been born.

Or he. It could be a he. They come in two flavors.

Carrots. To spite the chorus of relatives in my head, I pick up a bag of miniature carrots that are smaller than my little finger – luxury carrots, as if buying them will make some important change in Krys's life. As if the pattern she needs to break is the same pattern I once did.

At home I unload the groceries and look up a pot roast recipe in Peg's cookbook, but all I have to do is glance at it to call up my grandmother's recipe, exactly the way she wrote it out for me in those weeks after my mother died, using one sheet of notebook paper for pot roast, one for meatloaf, one for pan-fried chicken, one for hamburger hot dish. All neat, all separate, all unchangeable. If you do these things in this order, everything will come out right.

"You're the woman of the house now," she told me.

As if any woman would do. As long as her son was looked after and she didn't have to do it herself.

I was twelve and big for my age. If I did these things, it would all turn out right. She showed me how to sear the meat before I added the vegetables, how to peel the onion, how to wipe my eyes without rubbing onion juice into them. She showed me how to sort the laundry, how to pin it on the line.

"Your father needs you," she told me before she left. "You can't throw all your time away riding that bike anymore."

I didn't have a bike. Someone had stolen it off the front porch when my mother was still alive and she'd said it would teach me to take care of my things – did I think someone was downtown handing bikes out for free?

I didn't tell my grandmother that. She already had her doubts about me. I could read them in the tilt of her head when she looked at me, the way she sucked her breath in, the way she let it out in a sigh just before she showed me how much salt to add to the water before bringing it to a boil or how to spit on my finger and tap the iron to make sure it was hot. It all said, You're not what I had in mind but we'll have to make do.

Kids know these things. All the secrets we think we're keeping from them – one deep breath and they know them all.

I followed each of my grandmother's recipes. Sear the meat, add the vegetables. I wanted to show her I could do it. I sorted the laundry, hid my father's jockeys under the pillowcases and sheets so I could pretend not to see the sagging knit, the yellowed thread. When he was too drunk to unlock the front door, I crawled out of bed to let him in. I don't remember how long it took, but at some point I noticed that it wasn't all coming out right. My mother was still dead. My grandmother hadn't come back to see that I was what she had in mind after all. And whether he was drunk or sober, whether he was at home, at work or at the bar, my father had left me. We were sinking: he was, I was, the house was. So, one step at a time, I started mangling the recipes. I undercooked, I overcooked, I mismeasured. All I wanted, unless I've changed things around in my memory, was to have him ask what was wrong, but when he didn't I pushed further and further away from what my grandmother had written out for me. My pot roast had more salt than potato chips. If I'd loaded my meatloaf into a catapult, I could have demolished a brick wall. It's not easy to ruin something once you know how to cook it right. It takes determination. It takes character. I took a kind of pride in ruining our food, and my father shoveled in everything I fed him the same way that he drank, as if it was one more lousy job and why should he expect to like it? Poor sullen son of a bitch. It's taken me until now to understand that he must have been missing my mother, that what I saw was his form of mourning, just like salting and singeing were mine.

So now I move through what was Peg's kitchen more than it was ever mine, looking for flour to dredge the meat in, spice jars with actual labels on them, all the things I never had to find while Peg was alive. She was the cook. All I had to do was eat and clean up.

I litter the counters with everything that gets in the way of my search, and it comes to me, like a place I used to know and haven't thought of in years, that before my grandmother left, before I gave up on my father, before I decided that being Little Suzy Homemaker would kill me, I liked cooking. It comes to me that this is something I could have done for Peg, and I feel all the loss I was looking for yesterday, when I lowered her clothes into their black plastic coffins. She'll never walk in the back door and find me cooking pot roast. She'll never know that I'm capable of this form of love. I kept that from her. I kept it from both of us.

If Peg has flour tucked away anywhere, I can't find it, so I skip that step and hope I don't wreck anything. I don't trust my innovations, even when they're well intentioned. I sear the meat, add the vegetables, let it all simmer while I clear up the mess I've made.

Most of what you do when you cook pot roast is wait, so I sit at the kitchen table reading more of the morning paper than interests me. I work the crossword puzzle and poke at the meat every so often, as if poking was one of the steps in my grandmother's recipe. As far as I can tell, not having dredged it in flour hasn't hurt anything.

I've given up on the crossword by the time Krys comes in. I ask how she is and she says school sucks and she doesn't understand math.

"I don't either," I say, "but I can look at it if you want."

"Nah, I'll get Marco to explain it to me."

I don't argue. I don't know what Marco's math is like but it's not likely to be worse than mine.

Krys flops on the couch and channel surfs, flipping through a slice of laughter, music, a scream, voices, applause. I wonder, if Krys stays, whether I shouldn't get a TV for her room.

She settles for a while on cartoons – something with little duck-like voices.

By the time the meat starts to fall apart, the smell of it has worked its way into every corner of the house and I'm ready to believe that pot roast is what's missing in my life. Nothing about Megan's death has to stop me from eating meat. That was a reaction. It made no particular sense and maybe it's time to move on. I dish up two plates and call Krys in, but all I have to do is slide into my chair for my portion to turn from food to dead cow pieces. I poke my fork at it a couple of times.

Megan, I think, *still claiming her share of my life after all these years*. I carry my plate to the stove and microwave one of my overpriced frozen veggie slabs.

"My mouth wants it," I tell Krys, "but my stomach doesn't. Or else it's the other way around. The point is, it's not a principled thing, I just can't eat it."

"I used to wonder how come you never ate meat."

"I just can't, that's all."

She nods as if I'd explained something to her.

"I don't mind what other people eat," I say.

Which is true. I watch her shovel in pot roast and it doesn't bother me.

"I used to want to be a vegetarian," she says.

"How come?"

"Cause I was a little shit. Cause I thought it'd be cool to, you know, have something you couldn't eat and then everyone'd have to figure out how to live with that. Actually, I still think it'd be kind of cool but the thing is you have to eat dead leaves and tree bark and shit, and it doesn't seem like it's worth it."

"Ya, well. It's food. You get used to it."

"I didn't mean it was shit—"

The microwave dings and I pull out my molded plastic tray of leaves and tree bark. Krys is done eating but she stays at the table to keep me company, and I realize that time's sneaking past without either of us saying anything. I've almost forgotten what it's like to keep up a conversation. You have to make noises, otherwise the other person thinks you want to be left alone.

It all seems like a lot of work in return for not damn much.

"I don't do it to hassle people," I say. "It's just something I'm stuck with."

"Still," she says.

Still. Still, she'd like a way to make people jump through hoops for her or still, she'd like a way to be who she is and not get a lot of grief over it. A little of both, maybe. Of course, she only knows the broadest outlines of who she is yet. I tear the film off my plastic tray and the steam that was trapped underneath rushes out and blends into the pot-roast-scented air.

"You're lucky," she says.

"I am, huh."

"You don't have parents and all that breathing down your neck."

"I don't, but it's not enough to prove your point."

I have some vague idea that I should tell her about the problems life has waiting for her – the ones she hasn't even begun to imagine – but what would be the point? Instead, I shovel in some prefabricated sustenance.

"Know what I've been thinking?" she says. "I've been thinking I might try to look for my mother. For, you know – for Deena. I mean, I always thought about doing that, but since I've been pregnant—"

She nods her head off to one side as if the end of the thought is too obvious to need words.

"It's like there's this whole chain of people leading up to me, and they all had to get pregnant so that I could, you see what I'm saying? It makes me want to talk to her."

She's looking at me intensely, willing me, I think, to tell her something about her mother.

"What do you remember about her?" I ask.

"I remember sitting on the floor while she brushed my hair. I was wearing this pair of – jeans, I think they were. With a flower—"

She raises one foot so she can point to the hem of her jeans, where the flower must've been. I remember how fragile she was then, with bones as light as a bird's, and how much damage we risk doing when we touch another person's life.

"I liked to rub my finger across it. I liked the way it felt."

She drops her foot to the floor.

"That's the thing, though. I don't remember much."

"You were pretty small."

"Tell me about her."

"What've Jude and Dex told you?"

"She's *my* mother. I have a right to know about her."

I nod, but before I answer I corner the last mouthful of leaves and bark against the edge of the plastic tray, bring it to my mouth, chew.

"And if you don't like what you hear?"

She shrugs. What did I expect her to say?

"I liked Deena. She had this great energy, she was fun to be around, all that kind of thing. You couldn't help liking her. And for a while we thought she was doing okay with you. The thing is, though, you never knew what to count on with her."

I stop for a minute, looking for something to say, and find I've been staring at the table.

"This one time – this was a while before she left – you and Kerri stayed with us for the weekend, and when we went to drive you home Deena wasn't there. I mean, nothing – no note, no neighbor watching for us to say she just ran to the store. Nothing. Kerri was too young to understand yet, but you just freaked, and it made us wonder if maybe something had happened before – maybe she'd left you on your own, that kind of thing. I mean, it wasn't just 'I want my mommy', you completely lost it, pounding on the front door, shrieking, and we're trying to tell you it's okay, she's just late, she'll be here—"

I hear myself talking and feel like I'm sitting off in a corner of the room, listening while some ponderous older woman drones on. I notice that she's not explaining this well. There's no way the words she's said will give Krys a sense of what it was like, but Krys is watching me with that tight-wound, undefended face of hers, as if every word of this matters. All I can tell by looking at it is how easy it is to hurt her, not whether I have yet. Or whether hurting her might do some good.

I have no idea how long Krys pounded at the door and wailed for Deena. Nowhere near as long as she seemed to, I'm sure. Peg went over and knelt down so she could talk to her, but instead of calming down Krys ratcheted up until I thought something in her throat would tear. Eventually Peg picked her up and carried her back to the car, and Krys kicked and howled like she thought we were going to murder her. I couldn't help thinking we'd get arrested for kidnapping, for child abuse, for god knows what.

"The thing is," I say, "she drank. I mean, I've got nothing against a drink or two, but she *drank*. It's not that she didn't love you. She did. I think it tore her heart out to lose you, but that didn't mean she was any kind of a mother to you. That was the thing—"

I let it trail away. It's not good enough. It never will be good enough, even though I think we were right.

A bit of silence settles over us. I remember how Peg and I convinced ourselves not to overreact. True, Deena hadn't been home. But by the time we got to our place, she'd left a message. Things do happen. She'd had a reason.

"My father drank," I say, as if this gives me the right to have chosen Jude and Dex for her over Deena. "Both my parents, actually. I know what it's like."

Krys carries her plate to the sink and turns to watch me, leaning the narrow scaffolding of her rib cage against the counter.

"She came back for us, though. Jude and Dex wouldn't let us go."

I've never been sure if she remembered that and I've never known if it was okay to ask.

"Like I said, she loved you. If she's still alive, she still loves you. She was also perfectly capable of forgetting all about you when the mood took her. That's the thing about kids: they get in your way. It's never simple. Loving your kid doesn't make you a good mother. It's necessary but it's not enough."

She folds her arms across her belly as if she needs to keep the baby from hearing this.

"You don't just drop your kids off for a weekend and disappear for six months."

My voice has gone up a notch – I can feel it – and I make myself drop it back down.

"Peg always figured she was playing out the family pattern. After your grandfather died – your grandmother didn't leave or anything but she pretty much left it up to Peg to raise Jude and Deena."

No reaction. I don't know if I'm giving away the family secrets or talking about an episode from some soap opera she never particularly liked. Maybe she hears it as a cautionary tale that I'm only telling because she's pregnant.

Maybe she's right.

"Jude and Dex weren't perfect, I know that, but at least you could count on them coming home."

I could say more here. At the edge of my brain is a speech about how they took her and Kerri in without twenty cents' worth of hesitation and never complained that life would have been simpler if they'd had just their own kid to raise. Every word of that speech is true, but lurking around the edges is the belief that she should shut up and be grateful because only the closest of blood relatives own the right to complain.

It horrifies me sometimes, the things I find in my head.

Her arms stay crossed and she offers no hint of gratitude. I'm not sure if I should be disappointed by this or glad Jude and Dex didn't make her think she owed them that. She looks past me toward the window in the back door – the same window I was looking through the night I heard she was missing. I'm ready for her to tear into me about Peg's and my part in keeping her from Deena and I'm reaching, half-coherently, for a way to tell her what her life would have been like if we hadn't done that, but I can't seem to find it.

Instead she says, "Do you know where she lives?"

She makes it sound offhand, as if she thinks she can sneak the information out of me.

"We never knew where she went."

She watches me – or I think she does. I'm watching the plastic tray, the table, my greasy fork, remembering how Peg wanted not so much to find Deena as to make sure she was okay, and I feel as guilty as if I really did know. My mind slides from there to the conversations we had about seeing my father. I always thought I should and at the same time I was convinced that if I did his life would suck me in and I'd never get away. I didn't decide not to see him, but I never went either.

"I can't help thinking I owe him," I said to Peg once.

She told me family wasn't a cash transaction.

"If you do look for her," I say to Krys when I can't stand any more remembering, "go into it slowly, okay? And don't expect a lot. Don't take off with ten bucks in your pocket and run halfway across the country to her, because you don't know what you'll find there."

When she doesn't answer, I look up. She's looking out the window again.

"I'm not saying don't look for her, only that you should be careful."

She's still looking out the window.

"It's just that I don't want you to get hurt."

And so I join the ranks of mothers, fathers, aunts, teachers, grandparents, all of us saying the same things: Be careful. Stay home. Stay safe. When I was in my twenties, I'd have said, Go. Pack right now. Hell, don't pack. Who needs clothes? The worst it'll be is a disaster and at least then you'll know. But it's easy to be brave when you don't know anything. All I knew was that staying in my father's house was a slow way of dying.

And the world back then was less brutal. Or I thought it was.

"If you're falling, you don't want to count on Deena to catch you."

When I go to bed, Krys is downstairs still, with the TV on and the phone glued to one ear, but she keeps it all quiet enough that with the door closed I don't hear her. This is easy, I decide. This works. In the dark, I replay bits of our conversation, reaching for something I wanted to tell her about safety and risk, but it slips out of my grasp the way a jar does on a high shelf, sliding backward as my fingertips scrabble against it. I rearrange my pillow and tell myself to forget it before sleep slips out of reach the same way, but my fingers start fumbling for it again the minute I settle down. It's about Deena. It's about Jude – the dullest of the sisters and the safest one, the one who took in two extra kids before she turned twenty-one, even if she might have gotten just a little smug about herself over the years.

Will it do Krys any good if I do figure out what I want to say? She'll find her own way. We all have to.

The glass turns against my fingers, slips away, and eventually I sleep.

In the morning I keep the volume down on the radio, and before I leave I set out cereal, a bowl, a spoon and the bottle of vitamins for Krys to find when she comes down. Not because she wouldn't find them on her own but to let her know she's welcome here, she doesn't have to sneak in the window. To let her know I don't begrudge her the food. I start planning what to cook when the pot roast is gone, although that'll take a while. My grandmother's recipes were based on a family of five. She didn't cut them down when she taught them to me and I don't trust myself to adjust them for my needs.

. . .

On Thursday a boy skulks in behind Krys, reminding me of the way she crept in behind Dex that first night. He's not hugging a pillow, but he's making damn sure not to call attention to himself. Which works about as well as yelling, Hey, don't look over here. He's skinny and tall, and his face has a young boy's sweetness still, a kind of light I find myself mourning the loss of already. He's brown-skinned, and, yes, I do notice this. I can't not notice it. I don't count it as either bad or good, but it does seem to carry weight with me: this is the boyfriend and he is indeed Black.

They head for the stairs and she does a drive-by introduction.

"This's Marco."

I tell him I'm glad to meet him and he smiles, looking as awkward as if I'd asked when the wedding is.

Krys, on the other hand, is trying to pull this off as if she's been bringing boys up to her room since she first got her period. Her face is open and smiling, reminding me of what good friends we are, how well we've always understood each other.

"We're going to do some homework," she says.

"Krys, your mother'll kill me if I let you upstairs together. How 'bout you work down here?"

"We were *gonna* leave the door open."

"That'll do."

Or I hope it will.

I turn the radio on to give us all the illusion of privacy, and I try to think of a single reason I shouldn't let them jump into bed together. She won't get any more pregnant, and unless he's sleeping with half of South Minneapolis she's already got anything he has to give. But I'm not brave enough to let them snuggle up together in my spare room. They'll have to freeze their butts off in the back seat of somebody's car the way I did at their age.

There's no good reason for this except that the culture demands it. Peg could have made her own rules if she'd lived, but I'm not a blood relative.

Jude comes by on the weekend, bringing a couple of crib sheets.

"They were on sale," she tells Krys, half erasing the gift.

I leave the two of them in the living room and take refuge in the kitchen, setting up the coffee maker even though I don't want coffee myself and haven't asked Jude if she does. It's something I learned from Peg: if you want to make a person feel welcome, you offer them something.

Out in the living room, Jude's chattering, packing Krys's silence full of words for fear something real might happen. Kerri's made some team or other, although what team gets swallowed up by running water, by the blower on the furnace, by the refrigerator kicking in. What I do hear is what Jude doesn't say: that Krys has moved out and life at home is going on without her. Everyone but her is living happily ever after. I move the coffeepot off the hot plate and fill first one cup and then another directly from the stream so I can interrupt before Jude causes any more pain. A few drops spatter and hiss on the hot plate between pot and cup.

I hand Jude her coffee and she sets it aside like a Mormon, not sure how this thing came into her possession.

"You want a pop?" I ask Krys.

She jumps off the couch and says she'll get it. For a second, I think she'll jackrabbit out the back door and stay away till Jude leaves, but she comes back, less eager, can in hand, and settles herself on the end of the couch opposite mine, leaving Jude sitting solo and upright in the recliner.

"So," Jude says.

I echo her: "So."

"You doing okay here?" she asks Krys.

"Ya."

Two notes, making it almost a question: What's it to you? maybe, or, What do you care?

"When are you coming home, then?"

"Didn't think you wanted me."

"Course we want you."

Jude slams this across the room like a tennis ball. I have a flashing image of Krys as a golden retriever, shortstopping the ball, taking the impact on teeth, tongue, jaw. We want you. Slam. How much of being wanted can one person take?

"What about Dex?"

"What about him?"

"He want me?"

"He's your father, what do you think?"

I hold the cup to my lips, tasting the heat. Krys twists her head aside and down. She doesn't say what we're all thinking but Jude argues with her anyway.

"He is your father."

Krys picks at a scab on her wrist, a pinching motion, rolling it, loosening the edges. She lets it go and shrugs.

"'F you like."

Jude turns to me.

"What'm I supposed to do with this kid? I say – what? – maybe three words and they're all three of them the wrong ones."

I shrug and fight the impulse to run for the kitchen and make a second pot of coffee.

Krys pokes the tab of her Coke into the hole and out. In. Out. I test the rim above the coffee with my lips. Too hot still. I wait for them to work out whether she's staying with me or going home, but they seem to have scared themselves away from the topic. The tab breaks off in Krys's hand and she slips it into the pocket of her jeans.

"I gotta buy some clothes," she tells Jude. "Everything's getting tight."

"Oh, sure. All you have to do is ask. We're just made out of money, your dad and me."

"Ya, well, I can't zip my jeans anymore."

She lifts the hem of her top to show us the open zipper, the pie-shaped wedge of belly, and I realize that I knew about this the night she moved in and didn't offer to buy her new pants. I can call up a perfect newsreel of the two of us emptying out Peg's closet, but I can't remember what was in my head to keep me from thinking about what she needed.

Later, I think. *When Jude's gone I can slip Krys some money*, and I should feel good to have found a mistake I can fix, but I don't.

"I took some of Aunt Peg's sweatpants but they're too big still."

"Hey, did I tell you to get pregnant?" Jude says. "Did I tell you to quit your job? There's a lot of things you're going to need, and we're not going to be able to pay for all of them."

"I kept throwing up," Krys says. "What'm I supposed to do, go, 'Would you like fries or a side of puke with that?'"

"Krys!"

"Well, am I?"

"There's other jobs in the world. You ever think of looking for a different one?"

"I'm *preg*nant."

"I *know* you're pregnant."

Krys turns her head toward the dining room, the stack-all-the-stuff-I-haven't-put-away room, clipping Jude neatly out of the picture.

"*I* worked till I was eight and a half months," Jude says, as if that was Krys's fault.

I raise the cup and sip steam in through my lips.

"You can't afford maternity clothes, what do you think it's going to be like once the baby's born?"

"Fine, then. I'll quit school. I'll work full time. I'll go on welfare."

"You will not quit school."

I try to stop listening but I can't. It's a skill I never learned. In my family even the fights were silent, which left me thinking that noisy families were happy. So I let Krys and Jude bump me across every pothole in the logic of their argument until I'm ready to throw the pair of them out into the snow.

At this point I realize that I have stopped listening. This is what normal people do. This is how they manage.

"This isn't getting us anywhere," I say, expecting for a split second that they'll be as happy to know this as I am.

"She's not leaving school," Jude says.

Krys shrugs, a tiny, insulting gesture that she makes with one shoulder and that means she's agreed, especially since she wasn't serious about it to start with.

Jude fishes her wallet out of her purse and counts what's inside.

"Here, I'll tell you what I've got, I've got thirty bucks and that's it. I mean it. Go to Savers, go to Goodwill. People go through their maternity stuff. It's like kids' clothes, you don't have time to wear them out."

Krys still isn't saying anything and Jude hears this as a complaint.

"Look, you're too good to wear used clothes, you get a job, you make do with one pair of new pants. I don't know how you manage this. If you're old enough to raise this baby, you're old enough to start solving some of your own problems. You want the money or not?"

Krys shrugs again and says, "Course I do."

"Thanks wouldn't hurt."

Krys grins.

"Ya, it would."

"Rotten kid."

Jude gets out of her chair to flap Krys on the head with the money – it's a sizable wad, made up mostly of ones – then she hands it over.

"Hey, thanks," Krys says.

They haven't solved a thing but it's easier to breathe in their vicinity.

Until Jude leaves by herself, I'm not sure whether Krys is going with her or staying with me.

On Sunday I come home from the supermarket and find my living room colonized by kids braiding each other's hair. They look up and say hello and are happy to have me say hello back and leave the room. I fit into that most foreign of all categories: adults. If they're polite enough, I probably won't bother them.

And I don't. I unpack the groceries and put them away while bits of conversation drift past me, the girls talking over and through each other and Marco sitting silent on the floor. It all seems to be about other conversations – someone said something to someone else. Teenage drama. Nothing I need to know. When the groceries are put away, I turn back to a package of ground beef that I left on the counter and I stare at it. I poke it with one finger. The plastic film gives, and so does the meat underneath, but it doesn't scream or squirm so I slice the film with a knife and peel it back with as little of my fingertips as I can manage. I'm like a kid reaching to touch a snake for the first time. I manage to flip the meat into the bowl without knowing for sure whether I touched it, and I use the tip of a knife to pry off the bloodied paper – a thick thing, like a diaper – that's stuck to the bottom, grabbing it with the rumpled plastic film in my other hand.

I throw out the plastic film and the ground beef diaper and wash off the fat that may or may not be on my hands before I set out the eggs, the breadcrumbs, the spices. My grandmother taught me to line them all up before I started.

I break the eggs into the bowl and they slide along the slanted slab of meat like something out of a horror movie – the exact thing the kid reaching toward the snake is afraid of touching. I measure the breadcrumbs and spices and dump them on top. They're immaculate. I will live for the rest of my life on dried food and clear water. I can't think how cooks bring themselves to eat at all.

The breadcrumbs hide the egg, but my grandmother's recipe is merciless – you don't stir it with a spoon, you stick your hands in it. I wash my hands again and push up the sleeves of my sweater, then I plunge my fingers in, scooshing them through cold slime. My stomach holds steady and I realize it's possible to do this. It's entirely possible to do this.

The girls laugh about something and I pause with my hands wrist-deep in raw egg and beef, understanding, for no reason I can explain, that I don't want to love this child.

I don't know how long Krys will stay with me and I don't know that I'll see them after she goes. Knowing that I could lose them both nearly chokes me.

I take my hands out of the mush and wash them again, running the water hot enough to cut the grease, and I dash up the stairs still drying my hands on the dish towel. Once the bedroom door closes behind me I wait to cry but the tears have gone. I take a few deep breaths, hold the damp towel to my face as if dampness would coax them out, then give up.

Fine. No tears, just me holding a damp dish towel and not loving a child I haven't met yet. That's natural enough. Isn't that natural enough? It's no more than a tadpole right now. If I have to, I'll learn to love it later, when it grows into something I understand.

The thing is, I don't want to love it later. I don't want to love it at all. The world can just stop producing children for all I have to offer them.

I fold the dish towel, thinking the kids will be less likely to notice it this way, and less likely to wonder why I'm running up and down my stairs carrying it. I don't want them to think I'm strange, or that I cry in the middle of making meatloaf, or that I don't love the tadpole. They can think of me as furniture if they like, or as nothing more than a backdrop for their own dramas, and that'll be fine. They can not think of me at all.

To hell with them, it's my house. I can run up and down the stairs all day carrying dish towels if I want to.

Before I get around to flaunting my dish towel down the stairs, though, I catch a quick, behind-the-eyes image of Krys's tadpole, and it looks so lonely swimming inside her, and Krys's love for it feels so sharp-edged and frightening, that it pulls at me, insisting that I owe it something. As if we could all get love by damn well demanding it. My throat tightens around the tears I can't cry and I still don't love it but I soften enough to think I could go through the motions. Maybe the motions are more reliable than the real thing.

It will be years before anyone knows the difference anyway.

On Wednesday, Jude calls to ask how things are going. She feels left out, she says. She wouldn't have thought she'd say this but she misses Krys and wants to hear everything I can tell her, so we meet at a coffee shop and I tell her Krys is fine, she's no trouble, I'm happy to have her, and this is true enough but I feel like I'm describing life with the Teletubbies, all fake-grass carpeting and little cooing voices, with a white picket fence that's made of plastic. I tell her about the kids coming by on Sunday, and about meatloaf and my grandmother's recipes. I skip over what they meant in my life, but it's enough to take us through our chocolate chip scones and halfway through our coffee. Then we hit one of those air pockets, those moments of silence where neither of us knows what to say next.

"Is there anything I should be doing?" I ask, because I can't help believing that someone knows.

"You're doing more than your share already."

I shake my head.

"I feel so helpless," I say.

"Welcome to the club."

We nod at each other. Oddly enough, I do feel like part of a club. The aging women's club. We can't save our kids from a damned thing, but, oh, the things we've learned.

"I'm wondering if things haven't cooled off enough for her to move home," Jude says.

"She's welcome to stay."

"I'll tell you, for a while there? Before she went and stayed with you? I was about ready to cut her loose, that's how bad it got. I'd started – well, I've got to think about the younger kids too. I can't have her going at them every time they take a breath. I can't let her take them down with her."

She looks at her hands.

"I've been – I don't know. I think we should try it again. I think *I* should try it again. I mean, whatever happens, I did promise Deena—"

I nod.

"Maybe we all just needed a break. I think if I can just get her and Dex – if I can just get them together once without anybody saying anything to anybody—"

I imagine them all in a room together, saying nothing. In an odd way it really is what she means: if we could all just not talk about the hard stuff.

She shakes her head.

"I'm not ready for this, and that's the truth. I mean, here the kids are, just about grown, and we're starting back with babies again. And she'll make a mess of it. I know she will. You know how I feel about abortion. Well, I talked to her about doing that, that's how bad it got. She wouldn't even discuss it. Same thing with adoption. She thinks she's going to make up for everything Deena did wrong."

She twists her empty plate and it's like a kid twisting the steering wheel on a carnival-ride car. She can turn the wheel any way she wants but the ride's taking her exactly where it would go anyway.

"I don't know. Maybe Dex and I should've done things some other way—"

She adjusts the plate a fraction to the right.

"We did try, though. I mean, we were *there*."

"You were. Not everyone would've done what you did."

"She has no idea what's involved."

"No one ever does."

I press my finger onto the plate and lick off a few crumbs. To hell with it. They were calling to me.

"Whatever you need, I'm available," I say, and she nods vaguely, as if I'd put no more thought into this than into saying hello, how are you, call if you need anything.

Two days later, Krys goes home to talk and I guess nobody says anything, because when she comes back to my house she doesn't actually tell me she's moving home but she does ask if I can give her a ride and then starts packing. When I go upstairs she has two pairs of Peg's sweatpants laid out, plus a couple of her shirts and sweaters. She asks if I'm sure it's okay and we pack them into a grocery bag.

I tell her I'll miss her and she looks awkward.

"The thing of it is," she says, and then can't figure out how to tell me what it is exactly.

"They're your parents," I say. "That's how it should be."

"I guess."

"You're welcome here anytime. So's the kid."

We're upstairs, her in the spare room and me in the hallway holding a clutch of bags, and neither of us seems sure how to get downstairs. She says thanks. I tip my head to one side like someone spilling water off the top of her head, meaning it's no big deal although I can't seem to say so.

I drive her home and walk into Jude and Dex's with her as if I need them to sign for the delivery, then I drive myself back to a house that's emptier than it was before she moved in. I roam through it, fold her blankets, strip the sheets off her bed and toss them on the floor, peer into the empty closet, which is nothing more than a simple box now, with a bar and bare hangers.

I close the closet door, pick the sheets up off the floor and find enough stuff in the laundry basket to fill out a load, then pour soap into the machine and stand over it watching water spill into the empty drum, spreading the soap powder out and dissolving it.

In the seventies, when I was trying to reconstruct myself as a liberated human being, I sometimes worked on believing that I could become anything. Not in the butcher-baker-candlestick-maker sense – I didn't kid myself that I'd discover a ballet dancer or a physicist hiding somewhere inside me, full-grown and ready to apply for jobs – but I did teach myself to notice small moments: the shimmer of light on a wall; the water pouring into the washing machine. I learned to enjoy them. On the strength of that, I was going to become the kind of person who lived each moment fully. It had nothing to do with drugs – taking drugs reminded me too much of my parents. It just all seemed possible.

It wasn't, of course. Everything that had ever happened in my life bumped around behind me like a tin can tied to the end of a cat's tail: my father's dirty shorts, my grandmother's ruined recipes, my mother tucked up in her coffin like a doll in a box. It clattered, it banged, and I ran faster to get away from it all.

But it also *was* possible. It was what allowed me to fall in love with Peg when the chance came. It was what let me trust myself to her fresh-brewed coffee and her incense, to her request for one good memory of my parents and her bed with its peacock scattering of cushions.

I distribute the sheets, the pillowcases and the underwear around the tub so the load will balance, and then I just stand there watching the water level rise.

Most of the time, in those years before I met Peg, I wasn't anything like happy but I was young enough still to believe in possibility, and from this distance possibility looks surprisingly like happiness itself. I've passed fifty and can see the underside of sixty well enough that I know where spiders have anchored their webs on the ceiling. I not only can't be a ballet dancer, I don't expect to have another relationship. Sometime after I hit menopause, my body pretty much forgot what the point of sex was. I missed it, but that didn't change anything: I couldn't get interested anymore. I was like someone who's had a stroke. All around me people were chatting away in a language I used to understand but for me it had turned into gibberish. I even tried hormones but I could still only catch a sentence or two. But Krys was right in a way, although it's not the way she meant. Even in our bad luck, Peg and I were lucky. We'd found other ways to love each other by then. We stayed together. When a sentence or two suddenly came clear to me, we ran upstairs because we knew it wouldn't stay clear for long. Peg made jokes about my short attention span, but we were grateful for the moments when I could focus.

You can't start a relationship that way, though. Or maybe some people can but I'm not one of them. That part of my life is over, and maybe it's for the best. I don't want anyone trying to fill Peg's place in my life.

The water running into the machine shuts off and the vanes start to twist. A sheet dances with the open back of a bra. It's not much of a dance, really – the surprise is that the clothes get clean at all – but it's enough motion that I could keep on watching. Instead, I make myself shut the lid and when I get upstairs I call an old friend, one of the last people to stop calling after Peg died, and I ask if she wants to see a movie this weekend.

Not all things are possible, but some are. The small things. The tiny transformations. The dry miracles.

Weeks go by and I don't hear from either Krys or Jude. Which is good, in a way. It means things are going well. Or going well enough. More weeks go by. Jude sends a thank-you card, and Krys has added a note at the bottom, which touches me even if it wasn't voluntary.

I make myself plan one thing to do each weekend. I see movies I don't care about with people I do. I lose twenty dollars playing poker. It all seems a bit sad and lost, but it's better than sitting home.

Weeks pass this way, and then more weeks. Jude calls to say Krys had an ultrasound and they think it's a girl. I thank her for letting me know. It makes me feel like family, although if I were family I wouldn't bother feeling that way. More time creeps past and then, as if it came out of nowhere, the temperature rises into the fifties and the whole city goes crazy with relief. I pass a cluster of girls wearing jeans and T-shirts, their bellies bare where the two don't meet, and no jackets, not even a sweater. They look painfully vulnerable after so many months in winter clothing. The snowbanks get smaller by the hour and the streets run with grit and meltwater. All day long I squirt the windshield and run the wipers but nothing keeps it clean and by the middle of my shift I have half a headache from squinting through lines of dried mud.

A woman comes from the back of my bus to complain about some kids making noise.

I tell her they're not hurting anyone.

"It's because they're Black, isn't it?" she says. "You don't want to say anything to them because they're Black. They get a free ride because they're Black."

"They're not hurting anyone."

She parks herself in the seat closest to the door so she can glare across the aisle at me, and she goes on glaring for a good twenty blocks before she gets off.

The next day I get called into the office about a complaint.

The assistant supervisor is a guy I knew when he was still a driver, and as supervisors go he's not bad, although that doesn't say much. He has a sour stomach and a stubble of brownish beard and he keeps a bottle of Tums on the shelf behind his desk, and another one of Maalox. He runs through the whole story of the woman, the kids, me, and it's all larger and louder than it was in real life. In this version, the woman sat across from me because it was the only place she felt safe, and who knows, maybe it was, but that doesn't make the threat real.

"It was a racial thing, Darrell. She was making an incident out of nothing and if I'd done what she wanted I'd have been helping her do it."

"You've been a driver a long time," he says. "You know how it works. Just use a little diplomacy. Let her know you're on her side."

"I'm not on her side."

"I don't give a rat's ass whose side you're on. Pretend you are. Jesus, Marge, just be nice to her, that's all I'm saying."

I shrug. I haven't fed him the line he wanted.

"You know I've got to write you up."

I stretch my legs out and fold my arms to say I don't give a rat's ass either.

"Go on, get out of my office."

I unfold myself in slow motion, just to annoy him. He reaches behind himself for the Tums. When I'm halfway out the door, he calls after me.

"Remember: diplomacy. Keep 'em happy."

"You keep 'em happy, Darrell. I'm getting too old to bother."

Behind me, I hear him sigh.

There was a time when being written up would have mattered to me. It would have made my stomach as sour as I've made his. The company runs on churning stomachs. It counts on our fear, but the thing is, I genuinely don't care anymore. If they fire me, I'll drive school bus, I'll drive cab, I'll deliver packages. It won't pay as well but I don't need much. I could strip my life down to the bare boards and not be unhappy about it.

I can get the union involved and probably will. If for no better reason than because it'll annoy Darrell.

I walk along a row of buses that loom over me like some kind of modern-day mastodons standing trunk to tail and think that I could walk away from the job tomorrow. I could walk away from my house, with its bare closet, and live the way I was living when I first met Peg. It would leave me with only an occasional twinge of regret, and maybe not even that.

The bus I'm passing is painted top to tires with an ad for the zoo and I run my finger along a gritty lion as I pass. You don't see an enclosure in the picture, just the lion, living in zooless freedom. It could go anywhere but chooses to prowl the zoo for our viewing pleasure.

I stop in the open garage door and inhale the smells of Minnesota's achingly short spring: the moist air, the thawing soil, and right at the edge of that the smell of oil and diesel, of cement and tires. I could be anything but I choose to stand here, balanced between renewal and the internal combustion engine, between freedom and the raw meat the keeper throws me.

I choose to drive home because where else is there to go? At the corner of Lake and Chicago, where I stop for a light, a woman crosses from the Mexican restaurant that just opened to the shell of what used to be a drugstore, and halfway across she breaks into a run, not because the light's changing but because the mood takes her, or because the spring air is filling her lungs and she can't stand not to. She's flying the way I always imagined that youthful hart in Peg's father's song would fly. She could as easily be dancing. She must be thirty or thirty-five, with mocha skin and a gauzy skirt, and I feel something for her that I can't name – a longing that has nothing to do with lust. I don't want to sleep with her, I don't want to be her, I don't even want to have been that beautiful when I was her age, because beauty's no good to the person inside it. It doesn't make you any happier when you're thirsty and you reach for a glass of water, it just makes you look that way to outsiders. The water, the glass, the distance between you and them are all the same.

Maybe what I want is to cross the street with that much joy flowing through my veins again. One more time in my life, I want to break into a run for the pure pleasure of running.

When I get home, I call Krys to ask what she needs for the baby and we make plans to go shopping over the weekend. When I pick her up, she's at that snake-that-swallowed-the-hamster stage – not huge yet but showing. A large snake. A small hamster.

"Things okay at home?" I ask when she has the seat belt adjusted around the hamster.

"Good enough."

It's a kind of non-answer, a shrug in words.

We drive to the store, find a car seat on sale and load it into our cart, then push our way through displays of strollers, baby carriers, changing tables, cribs – an entire world of objects you can only use for three months, for two years, but once you've seen them you can't imagine having a baby without them.

We stop to look at infant swings.

"Your mom had one of these for you," I say.

Krys touches it, using just two fingers, as if it was the same one Deena's hands had slipped her into.

"Some days it was the only thing that helped."

"Was I hard?"

"For a while."

She pushes a switch to one side and the seat rocks.

"Yours had a crank. You wound it up, it ran down, you wound it up – this is way better."

She watches the babyless seat swing backward and forward, imagining the perfect time she had with her mother before her memory was able to record it, and the time she'll have with her own baby, which will fill all the holes in her life. This baby she's carrying won't cry. Or if it does, Krys won't mind. She and Marco will get a place of their own. Twenty-dollar bills will flutter down from the sky, settling on their palms as lightly as butterflies. The child will be beautiful, with khaki skin, a starburst of curly hair, and startling green eyes. They'll live happily ever after. We'll all just get along.

I can't know what she imagines.

I watch the swing with her until she turns it off and we move on, past bassinets, lamps, mobiles, crib bumpers. If no one else gives her a swing and if we can't find one at a garage sale, I'll come back and buy this one.

Krys stops to touch the mane of a rocking horse with one finger. Her face is dreamy and soft. Her daughter's riding it. She's the poster child for happiness. Her clothes are perfect, the apartment's spotless, the laundry washes itself. Krys moves her hand to the hamster bulge, rubbing it in a kind of lullaby, and she's as beautiful doing this as the woman I watched running across the street. A youthful hart or roe. This is what all of us want: this moment, stretched out forever. But she lets her hand drop, the moment shatters and she's a kid again, with no idea how to raise a child, never mind support it.

And the baby will get herself born anyway. Krys will be the mother she'll be and the rest of us will watch the child, and without knowing it's happening we'll learn to love her. Even me. Even Dex. We're wired for that. We're helpless. We count up all the ways that people can leave us, all the ways that people aren't what we wanted them to be, all the ways that we're not what we wanted to be or what they need us to be, and with all our flaws we love them anyway.

It may not be good enough but it's what we have.

"Once the baby's born," I say, "you stay in touch with me, okay? I want to be part of her life."

She gives me an odd look, as if I'd explained that I'd like to be human.

"Well, ya," she says, in that two-tone Minnesota way, inviting me into this tiny joke.

5

I COME awake to the sounds of traffic and birdsong, to a slice of not-quite-daylight sky beside my blowing window shade, to the entire commerce of the early-morning city pouring through my open window. After the long sensory drought of winter it's as rich as chocolate, and a single word forms in my head: *enough*, meaning not the birds or the cars and buses, not the breeze flapping the shade, but the way I've moved through this past year without seeing, smelling, caring, and before I have time to think about it and lose the impulse toward motion I push myself out of bed and begin the day the way the living do when life allows it. I wash, I dress, I eat. I think of Peg. Over and over again, I think of Peg. I look into the dining room at the table where, in an unintentional tribute to her, I've dumped everything that didn't seem worth the effort of putting away. It's time for all of it to go: the torn envelopes, the plastic bag from Walgreens with nothing left inside but the register receipt, the cotton wadding from a pill bottle, the single winter glove, the half-used roll of Scotch tape. I sort through it all like an archaeologist of mourning, each layer marking a new stage of grief: denial, bargaining, whatever-I'm-missing, and I-never-meant-to-get-to-this-point, really-I-didn't, but in the opposite order. I throw away, put away, try to remember how it was that these two simple acts were so far beyond me, and my mind brushes the surface of my regrets as if they were a collection of polished stones, skimming here over a moment when I could have been kinder, stopping there to notice a way I could have let Peg know more of me. And inevitably I find Megan. Not in flames this time. I haven't slammed her against the dumpster yet. She's standing outside Peg's building in the cold, alive, unharmed, still a threat to everything we might make of our lives.

If I hadn't hit her, she might have lived.

If she'd lived, Peg would never have been free of her.

If I were making the choice again, would I hit her?

I would.

I think I would.

Even after all this time, I don't know how I could have caused less damage without letting her set fire to our lives.

I roll a pair of socks together and set them on the stairs to take upstairs next time I go, then come back to the table, where I seem to be sorting through all my failings, but with their edges rounded, their shapes familiar and almost welcoming. I'm grateful for them all. I have these regrets. Without them I'd be a different person, with a different life.

On the lowest layer, resting on the grain of the table itself, I find a bottle of pills with Peg's name on the label, a T-shirt of mine, folded and apparently clean, and Peg's key chain, which I slip into my pocket, thinking not that she'll find a way to come back and use it but that she was always the one who drew me home, and that in one way or another she still can.